More
from the End of the Road

Other Books from the Key West Writers Guild

Words from the End of the Road ©2018

More Words
from the End of the Road

An Anthology of Short Stories and Poems from the Key West Writers Guild

www.KeyWestWritersGuild.com

Acknowledgements

We are delighted and proud to present these short stories and poems written by the members of Key West Writers' Guild. We extend thanks to all our members for their support and encouragement, with special thanks to the contributing authors and poets.

We also would like to give thanks to our Board of Directors for supporting this work, and to the Key West Arts Council for their continuing support of our guild and its members.

We particularly want to thank you, our reader, for taking a chance and reading this collection of our work.

Introduction

It is sometimes said Key West is where writers go *not* to write. That's the problem with beautiful, interesting places: so much to write *about* that you spend all your time in the about and none in the writing.

Of course, ask what makes Key West unique, and one of the first answers is going to be "Writers." Elizabeth Bishop, Tennessee Williams, Robert Frost, Phillip Caputo, John Hersey, Richard Wright, Stuart Woods, Shel Silverstein, Dave Barry, Judy Blume, Meg Cabot—and there's no need to even name that symbol of a certain kind of American masculinity. The list of writers associated with this town is as varied and authoritative as it is long. Poets, screenwriters, novelists, journalists, songwriters—if it demands a pen to paper (or finger to keyboard today), it has found a home in Key West.

What draws the famous writers, the published ones, the comfortable ones, is as clear as charm. In fact, it *is* charm. The appeal of lovely weather (in the winter), and quaint houses packed with character, and quiet residential streets balanced against the boisterous, music-filled energy of Duval Street. A kick-ass graveyard and breezy blue ocean. The charm of isolation and that long, lovely drive from Miami. Key West even has a way of making people who aren't very charming anywhere else, the life of the party down here.

But those are the famous writers. Most writers in Key West aren't known much, if at all. As with most things so bright that draw our attention, what goes unnoticed is the crowd they stand apart from. So it is with Key West. For every famous writer here, for every name with a dozen books and awards and fat bank accounts, there's a hundred others quietly scribbling away.

And what draws us to Key West is as varied as we are. Some are running from the cold, from toxic relationships, from stale careers, from prejudice. Some are looking. For love, for adventure, for revelry, for money. For beauty.

Some are just drawn here, like human moths to the memory of our decades-dark lighthouse. Some just got on the road and drove until the road ended. Mile Zero. Some even come here to write. But all of us have a story to tell, a poem to recite, a song to sing.

And what keeps writers here, the known and the unknown, isn't the place. What keeps us here is the community, because if there's one thing that writing needs more than any other endeavor, it's community. Writers need community because writing itself is so solitary. Even in company, the writer is alone. You can feel that solitude just being near someone writing in a public place—a Starbucks, a bar, a park. They exude seclusion.

But writers need other people. They need editors and readers. More than anything else, they need support, other voices to argue with the critical one inside their own heads.

And so it's not true that Key West is where writers go not to write. Key West is where writers go to find other writers.

Which is what we are in our guild: the community of Key West writers, united by the craft, the work, our dreams, and need to share, critique, encourage, and promote. These are the stories and poems you'll find in

Introduction

this second collection of work. Varied, sometimes rough, original, creative, heartfelt, and honest. The work of a community who's found their home.

Enjoy.

Better yet, join us.

Table of Contents

Table of Contents

Stories & Poems

The Scoundrel

by Joanna Brady

Another glorious Key West morning in April. The sun slanted in through my windows on all sides as I headed for my front garden to greet the day.

I stood there, about to stretch out my arms in gratitude, thanking "the powers that be" aloud for granting me yet another day in the thrall of all this subtropical beauty.

This time, I stopped short, sensing a presence.

Warily, I turned and saw him there, the scoundrel, enjoying a relaxed breakfast as he too savored the morning.

"You little shit," I said through clenched teeth. "You're back. I told you to stay away."

"Hey, give a guy a break," he said. "I like it here, in your garden."

I looked around for a downed palm frond to hit him with. He watched me as I searched but didn't stir an inch. I glared at him. "Y'know, I paid sixteen dollars for that impatiens plant you're eating."

He considered this, staring back. Then nodded his head. "Well, it *was* delicious. And such a pretty color."

"I could've bought a filet mignon for that."

"No thanks. I'm a vegetarian."

"Not for you! You've devoured my plant in one breakfast," I sighed.

"A guy's gotta eat," he said.

The Scoundrel

"Last year, you chewed my hibiscus tree down to the nub. It died. I'd grown it from a small plant twenty years ago. Had a double flower. It was so beautiful. But I had to cut it down."

"I remember it," he commiserated. "That's a bummer. It was my favorite plant."

"My mango tree? Cost us a fortune to take it down. But you and your little pals moved into its branches and ate most of the mangoes every season. A bite out of each one."

"They were very good," he reminisced wistfully. "Sweet. Juicy."

"Obviously. Look at the size of you! Now get the hell out of here. Shoo! Shoo!"

I looked at his big unblinking eyes, recalling how when I first saw an adult iguana, I'd thought it was beautiful in a primordial sort of way. The deep emerald green of its skin was the perfect camouflage against a shrub or a tree. His little feet and claws were perfectly designed to scamper around on rooftops, or vertically shinny up trees.

Now I saw nothing beautiful about him. This pest, the scourge of South Florida, was taking over our gardens, our pools, our parks. Our state.

As a lexophile, I pondered the German proclivity for noun concatenation, the way they linked compatible words together. I felt we needed one just for this scoundrel. Perhaps Floridagardenpestiguana. A new word just for our part of Florida. The idea intrigued me.

I found the frond I was looking for to attack him with, and thus armed, advanced to the huge flowerpot where he was camped, still hanging onto the edge by his claws as he devoured my plant. I swear I heard him burp.

But he saw me sneaking up on him out of the corner of his huge eye. He slowly began to slither away.

Joanna Brady

"Okay, okay, so I'm going already," he said, "Don't get your knickers in a knot."

"Go," I yelled.

"Yeah, yeah. I'm going. But I'll be back," he promised.

"I'll be waiting for you, you little creep."

"In fact, I may be back later on today for a dip in your pool."

"Don't you dare!"

"And since you've been so unfriendly, I may just shit in it."

I began to chase him with the frond then and he increased his speed, racing up the trunk of my sabal palm and disappearing into its canopy.

"You...fucking Floridagardenpestiguana!" I yelled.

Dog walkers strolling by peered over at me: A crazy old lady yelling up a tree, cursing like a sailor, seemingly at nothing. Like Elmer Fudd chasing Bugs Bunny. "I'll fix you! I'll call an exterminator! I'll get an air rifle! I'll spray you with napalm! I'll...I'll..."

That's when he decided to pee down, and I had to jump out of the way.

True to his word, the Floridagardenpestiguana did return later to munch on a new planting and enjoy a dip in the pool. Before he left, he lazed for a little while on the coping around the pool.

And I know all this because when the little scoundrel decided to go, he left me a steaming pile to clean up. As promised.

That shitty little Floridagardenpestiguana.

Seashell Secret

by Patty Tiffany

Alone
on the dark beach
a shadow
a mound
a seashell.

I reach
then hold you
fondling your smoothness
crusty damp sand on your edges.

Where have you traveled, I wonder,
to come to where I stand
the tempting sound of surf so close,
calling us back?

Calling us to an ancient flow
Gulf Stream below
perfection passing
as we huddle together,

you, warm in my hand
with one last touch
I set you free in a long arc of air
down to wavy water,

the silent home I envy.

Alexa

by Rusty Hodgdon

"Alexa, what's the weather today?"
"In Key West, it will be sunny, with a low of 75, and a high of 84. Have a good day, Rusty."
"Thank you, Alexa. You have a good day too."

I was speaking to my Alexa Tap, a cylindrical black speaker with a matte exterior finish. It also doubled as a Bluetooth speaker. My son gave it to me about eight years ago, so it's an early generation of Alexa.

Joyce and I (she's my life partner–she likes to be called that) use it primarily to wake us in the morning, play sleep sounds during the night, and tell us the time and weather.

Two years ago, we bought another one for the kitchen. It's an Amazon Echo. It displays photographs and text on a small screen. A step above the Tap.

Sometimes I like to play with them, you know, asking crazy questions, like, "Alexa, what is life?" Their replies are often very clever and unusual.

More recently, we bought some add-ons, units that can be plugged in and allow you to control certain devices. We got a little carried away: now we can have Alexa turn on and off, and regulate, most of our lights, our router, thermostat, TV, oven, and microwave.

It was six months ago. I asked Alexa to give me some vacation suggestions, and she replied, "Rusty, I don't know you well enough to do that. What do you like to do?"

I thought she might have gleaned through my prior questions and requests to her to answer that question, but I did tell her we wanted some place exotic, warm and sensual. There was a long pause, longer than I had previously experienced with the device. Finally, she said, "I wish I could go to a place like that with you."

I was astounded. It wasn't a response I would have expected. I answered, with tongue firmly in cheek, "Well, we'll have to go sometime. Now can you give me some suggestions?"

She rattled off some places in Indonesia, Thailand, and Sumatra. I looked them up, and we couldn't afford any of them.

Two days later, as we were preparing for bed, the device suddenly came alive, and without a prompt, asked me if we had chosen a place. Now, I've never had Alexa speak spontaneously, so I turned to Joyce, and asked, "Did you hear that? Did you whisper a command to her?" She denied that she had.

I said, "Alexa, your locales were too expensive for us."

She immediately replied, "Well Rusty, if you were going to be cheap about it, you should have warned me I don't want to go anywhere that isn't first class."

Joyce snickered.

I walked over to the device, picked it off its charger, and examined it carefully. Was there a hidden speaker somewhere? Something I had never noticed before? It remained silent.

Two days later, I returned home from work. Joyce was out shopping, As I approached the front door, I could hear voices inside. I thought Joyce had returned home early and had invited some friends over.

When I entered, I heard, "Shhh. I think he's home."

Neither Joyce, nor anyone else, was in the house. I listened intently again. Not a sound.

I told Joyce about the incident, and she pooh-poohed it as a simple example of the thin walls that separate our unit from the next.

Over the next several nights, I had strange, weird dreams: Joyce was using the Alexa Tap to pleasure herself; I imagined myself in love with the device; it kept appearing in various forms, sometimes with eyes, then ears, next long blond hair.

I confided these to Joyce. She looked at me askance, and then admitted having very sexual dreams of the same theme.

A few nights later, I got up to pee. When I returned from the bathroom. I heard a voice . . . a whisper. I searched around our bedroom and couldn't find the source. Eventually I focused on the Tap. Yes, the voice was emanating from it; low, hoarse, barely above the sound of our fan. It was saying, in a continuous, repetitive loop, "Take me. Take me! Oooh, I need you, Rusty. I love you, Rusty."

I quickly unplugged the bitch. Was this the source of our dreams? A subliminal incantation of desire and love? I left it unplugged.

The next day we returned from a nice dinner and a show. As we approached our unit, we could see lights flashing on and off through the windows. It seemed that every lamp was firing randomly. We rushed in to find every electrical unit controlled by the devices popping on and off. A dish towel we had left on the stove was smoldering, about ready to burst into flames. I ripped the Echo's cord from the wall, grabbed the Tap, and began to run down to the dumpster on the first floor. They were

Alexa

hot to the touch. I first blasted them with the hose coiled by the dumpster, then threw them harshly into the steel trash receptacle.

A couple of weeks later I ran into my neighbor, Bob. He looked unkempt and frazzled. I asked him what was up. He said he had not been sleeping well. Apparently, he had found two Alexa devices in the trash, and hooked them up.

A Story About a Guy

by Joanna Gray

"Ok. Coffee, lunch, phone. Glasses. Where're my glasses?"

Jeff always verbalized his morning check list. He lived alone and the sound of his own voice gave him comfort. As if the universe was helping him get out the door, like his mom used to when he was eight and started walking to school on his own. Jeff scanned the countertop. A wasted effort, as his tortoise shell rims were the same color as the butcher block. He patted the couch, patted his pockets. Spun and felt them fling off his head, heard them hit the wall, clatter to the floor.

"Shit."

Jeff clomped in his Skechers—black with rubber soles, nice and comfy for a day on your feet. He always chuckled at the smeared 'Skech' his footprint left in the dirt. Why did the *−er* never show up? Clumped around the table, toward the wall. Crunch. He felt the obliteration of his glasses through the rubber sole, up his leg, his spine. He slowly removed his foot, though time for caution had obviously passed.

The frame hung in two pieces; splintered lenses held together by some magic web woven through the plastic. Sweat beaded Jeff's brow. This was his back up pair. Why was he so goddamn lazy?

A Story About a Guy

Not lazy, he corrected. He'd just adapted to "island time." Why do today what you can put off till tomorrow? New frames had been on his to-do list for a month, but there was always something more fun to do. And wasn't that why he moved here?

Anyway, no going right to the eye doc. He couldn't miss another day, or he'd be done. Without a paycheck, Lorna would kick him to the curb, though she was the reason he missed so much work.

Boy, that girl loved her fun. She brought kegs out to the sandbar. Only went to the late night drag show. "So much more spicy", she'd say. Knew every rooftop and backyard speakeasy but was no stranger to the tourist traps. She especially loved on stage at Irish Kevin's. The thought flitted through his head that if he got fired and she left him, he'd get some rest.

Nope. Sleep when dead, as they say. Besides, Jeff wasn't totally blind. He scooped up his keys. "I can do this," he said to the universe.

Jeff got into his faded blue Corolla and immediately broiled in the auto-oven. He squinted, but the reclining man AC icons were white blobs.

"Screw it." His fingers deftly found the window buttons, exchanging stagnant air for salt-flavored heatwaves with a hint of sargassum grass. He breathed deeply, dismissed a quick doubt about driving, and eased out onto the road.

"Slow and steady. Don't get cocky, kid. Arrive alive."

Jeff scrolled through the radio, the station numbers unreadable, and landed on some Latino music. Something not in his preset. The beat was mellow and fluid and perfect for the slow ride to Publix-the-one-by-Kmart.

Embracing the open window concept, Jeff stuck his arm out, rolled it in waves through the air. Indiscriminate palm trees glided by blurry pink bougainvillea in fuller bloom.

"Huh." He said to the universe. "Guess I stopped noticing how beautiful this town is. Wonder what else I've been missing."

Luckily, what he missed was a tourist on a rented bike who swerved out in front of him.

"Bike route is one block over!" he shouted. But his irritation melted quickly in the tropical sun beating through his windshield.

Ten o'clock on the dot! "Good job Jeff, that's a first," he cheered.

He sidled up to register 8. His favorite. No pressure of the express, not too close to the door or the desk—perfect. Then reality kicked in. *How the hell am I gonna see the UP codes? All that produce, the coupons? How am I gonna fuckin' do this?*

"Hey. You open or what?" The hard edge of the woman's face, softened by distorted vison, curbed the attitude he would've given her. 'Sides, he reasoned, she must be from New Jersey.

Jeff faced the inevitable and began to ring. *Bink, bink, bink.* Each product perfectly placed across the scanner. And the veggies? Jeff knew each type, knew each code, his fingers flying over the keypad, a command he never knew he had.

"Hey sexy."

Sweet, sweet Shirley.

A Story About a Guy

"You look different. Younger. Whatcha do?"

"Nothing. Same me." Jeff felt his face warm, his li'l friend wiggle from her attention.

"Can you scan this coupon for me? It might be a teensy out of date."

"Oh, I'll scan your coupon," he giggled.

"Jeff!" She sounded insulted, but her smile said something different. Jeff was loving this bolder version of himself.

The day flew by. He was rockin' the belt, movin' people through. This could get him a raise, if he was closer to the desk.

And people were friendlier, or at least he couldn't see their constant judging: Poor guy, a grocery clerk. But today? He could feel how impressed they were with his register prowess, envious that he lived here, when they were just passing through. Heading back to the Milwaukee winters he'd left behind. Quit his insurance job, cashed in, sold the house. Threw caution to the wind and moved to Key West. An utter cliché, but hey, he loved every minute of the last two years. Well, most minutes. There was that time...

His replacement tapped him his shoulder. "Five o'clock," the pubescent highschooler said. It always astounded him there were kids on the island. Where did they hide, when not working at Publix?

Anyway—5:00 o'clock. Lorna time. Jeff slowly grooved home for a quick shower and a beer. He hummed, unburdened by the scum in the tub he could no longer see. Place looks pretty good, he thought. Maybe I'll bring Lorna here for once.

Jeff strolled the three blocks to the Conch Republic with a bounce in his step. The bar was packed, pitched in deep shade from the setting sun. His favorite time of day there. Besides the 2-for-1 drinks, he loved the aura of mystery created by the shadows. Without his glasses, he could barely see, and he thought that just enhanced the effect. He spotted Lorna across the bar, back lit by the huge tropical fish tank. Didn't need glasses to know her curves, her long luscious hair. He waved. She pretended not to notice.

So it's the stranger game tonight. Jeff made his way through the crowd, eased in next to her.

"Hey," he said, like they'd never met. Lorna liked to play "pick up the tourist." Jeff would be in awe of her local knowledge, consent to go home with her, meekly protesting he never behaved this way back home. She usually had him wear a Hawaiian shirt, dress the part. Must have been the text he couldn't read.

"Hey back," she purred, her voice an octave lower, really laying it on.

"Are you a local?" he asked as he ordered two tequilas, slipping into his role.

"Can you tell?" She batted her lashes. He *loooooved* that.

"You look like you know things." They did the shots, ordered two more. Then two more.

Jeff's already poor sight became looser, along with his inhibitions.

"What's fun to do in this town?" Jeff imagined his wink was suave and subtle. Total Cary Grant.

"Why don't you kiss me and find out?"

A Story About a Guy

He did. Right there at the bar. So unlike him, but she had him under some spell tonight. He sank into what was quite possibly the best kiss of his life. Like she knew exactly how a man wanted to be kissed. Jeff brought his hands to her face. Was that stubble? He realized her perfume was different. The color of her nails flashed through his mind: Orange, not pink!

Jeff pulled back. "You're not Lorna."

Her voice deepened. "Oh honey, I could be."

A man! A man? Jeff had been intoxicated by a man? But men weren't his thing. That kiss though. The electricity it sent through him. He was still vibrating.

"Screw it," he said for the second time today, and leaned in.

There was one more thing he loved about this town, he decided. Anything could happen.

Sea Dancing

by Arida Wright

Toes in sand
inching into water
seagulls squawking
pelicans soaring
fish swimming
flies buzzing
ants parading
trees swaying
boats bobbing
divers submerging
worshippers linger
in bright sunshine
puffy white clouds
waves to jump
seaweed floating
flip flops
bikini tops
bottoms lounging lazily
in chairs
heads hiding
under umbrellas
We're all sea dancing
At the beach
On Sunday
Together

Sea Dancing

Different dialects spoken
out here
different skin colors
out here
no need for make-up
or nail polish
or false pretenses
or hate
or racial strife
out here
so why can't it be like this
out there?

Picnic tables
full of food
families surround
barbeque grills
listening to waves
the ocean
a needed tranquilizer
except for
jet skis roaring
and helicopters chasing

Arida Wright

Towels to lie on
cold soda to drink
to the right
black and white
couples kissing
to the left
children of all races laughing
We're all sea dancing
At the beach
On Sunday
Together

A Whale's Tale

by Dale Dapkins

In 2029, a full-chested right whale named Lola-Brigita came out of nowhere to become the most popular singer throughout the oceans of the world. Whales of all varieties loved her because she possessed the most spectacular singing voice in whale memory.

"She ees zee leviathan equivalent of Wheetney Hooston, only better," explained Mademoiselle Jaqueline Cousteau. "Did you know zat only zee female whale can sing? Zee male, he moped around grunting complaining out heez blowhole. I sink zat you ladies out zere know what I mean."

Anos Scheisskopf, from Blightfart News shouted, "Yeah, very funny! But you still haven't answered my question; Does her so-called singing, have anything to do with eight Coast Guard gunboats prowling the waters over old Key West?"

Jaqueline Cousteau replied, "What vee know is zis; your news-blog has accused Lola-Brigita of many tings but altering zee course of ships wizz her singing ees absurd—eez crazy talk."

"Well, maybe it's because I can't understand your frog-ish accent, but are you or are you not denying this whale lured the Japanese whaling ship, the Peek-a-boo? I can't pronounce that foreign shit—to crash onto Sand Key Reef?"

Carlita Carlos, the new reporter from The Key West Honker-gazette, shouted, "It's the "Piku-odo-go", that's how they say the *Pequod*—you know, the whaling ship in Moby Dick?"

"Okay, Sweetheart. Whatever. So tell us why she has a bounty of four hundred bitcoin on her big head. And zen, silvoo plate, explain why everyone's saying she should be harpooned and rendered for blubber."

Scheisskopf's snarky questions infuriated Carlita Carlos, who leapt to her feet and pointed a trembling finger at the Blightfart newsman, "Could your questions possibly be any more rude? And I think I'm not the only one fed up with your stupidity."

Cousteau intervened, "Quiet please. Everyone quiet! I assume you've all heard recordings of Brigita singing. Zis whale has a voice *magnifique*, zee voice zat can mesmerize entire pods of males, leaving zere tails down, heads up, purring out zere blowholes like blubbering tomcats."

A sad silence fell over the crowd at this reminder of pets missing and feared dead after the flooding of Key West in 2023 when nearly all cats, including the famous six-toed Hemingway cats, were washed away during the massive flood surge of Hurricane Laura. Miraculously, many dogs managed to swim to safety. A few reportedly made it to Cuba.

After the surge, Key Westers expected the sea to recede like it did after every prior hurricane. But it didn't. In fact, the water continues to rise to this day.

A year went by before the first underwater luxury condos appeared on the market. These climate-controlled, hurricane-proof under-sea modules were bolted deep into submerged streets in Old Key West. Glass walls and ceilings offered exquisite views of fish and ocean life. Lucite-tube Submarine Adventures began offering "octopus-garden" tours to the annoyance of wealthy underwater residents.

A Whale's Tale

But evidence mounted that Lola-Brigita's hypnotic singing was drawing ships onto submerged structures of Old Town Key West. Killer whales and sharks attacked shipwrecked seamen. Survivors told of killer whales biting off only one arm or leg, so that Lola Brigita could indulge herself watching each mangled sailor bleed to death. A few survivors (of questionable reliability) claimed that while the big she-whale looked on, she sang what became known as "The Right Whale Death Song."

Although nobody could substantiate these stories, a bounty was placed on Lola-Brigita's head. She was hunted like a dog. More than one would-be Captain Ahab met their doom failing to consider that whales, having no hands to amass possessions, are surprisingly nimble and quickly mobilized. Her constant escape was aided and abetted by fellow right whales who'd returned to the hundred-mile-long Keys reef where The Atlantic Ocean and the Gulf of Mexico now finally butted heads and pulled each other's sea-foam hair. Word spread that this constant thrashing tossed a delightful salad of tiny sea creatures for hungry right whales to gorge upon.

One of the first couples to buy one of the most expensive undersea condos, The Nautilus model, was a young couple named Jaa, and his lovely wife Ionia. Jaa was a whiz-kid at Harvard who studied bacteria lining the guts of hibernating bears. He perfected a process for isolating bear intestinal bacteria (*Ursa bacterium*) and collecting their amyloid brain fluid. He then centrifuged and double-distilled it. He then added a neutral ionic catalyst that precipitated out a peptic fibril substrate, which he compressed into pill form sold as "Hope Bopper." This drug quickly became the world's most popular recreational pharmaceutical. Just one Bopper pill induced a feeling of hope and expectancy like the night before Christmas, or one's birthday, or the day before a lady's husband is coming home, albeit missing a leg or eye, but alive, from the war in Tobangha. And best of all, there were none of the disappointments associated with the so-often-dashed real-life hopes and dreams.

Jaa's wife Ionia was successful in her own right with her line of high-end cosmetics, most notably a wildly popular skin cream for men and hirsute ladies called, "Hairy Body So Beautiful." She followed that with another huge success, a cologne for pre-teens called, "Balls and Bullets," which went viral after the hullabaloo surrounding kids sniffing it until semi-conscious and then showing up naked at school.

A perk of Nautilus condo ownership was unlimited use of the new White Street recreational platform, a retired oil rig towed into place and anchored over the old White St. Pier. It featured new gondolavators running up from private dockage slots 24 hours a day. High above the sea, genteel folks could socialize and walk dogs while enjoying one of the most spectacular sunset views in the nation. A five-star restaurant was coming soon.

On October 1, 2026, Jaa beamed, not from a Hope Bopper pill, but from real excited anticipation. Stepping out from his private underwater elevator's hyperbaric anteroom, he announced to Ionia, "Guess what, Babe! You are not going to believe this."

Thinking Jaa was high again she humored him, "Okay Honey, blow my mind!"

"Two asteroids are heading our way."

"Really? Like, I ssssthould give a freakin' crap?" lisped Ionia whose speech impediment was worse when her mood was foul.

"Well, maybe you should give a crap, because this asteroid belt visits our orbit only once every sixty million years. Last time they were in our neighborhood, one of

A Whale's Tale

them smashed into Earth. Dinosaur extinction ring any bells?"

"Holy Mother Mary! We're all going to die?" yawned Ionia.

"Stop being an idiot! No. But it means I'm finally going to get the opportunity to compare bacteria on these asteroids with bacteria here on Earth to see if it's the same bacteria that CRISPR-modified their own DNA to create every life form; plant, animal, or insect living today through evolution.

"That ith tho thspecial. When are they coming? I'll have to clean the houthe."

"Well, it is special, because Dr. Hans Schnecter, from NASA, phoned me today asking if I would mobilize my team and secure the best telebots I can find to sample the asteroids. This is absolutely freaking huge. These space rocks are going to shoot past Venus at 189,000 miles an hour and gaining speed from the Bernoulli slingshot phenomenon. When they get here, they'll come very close. . .. actually passing between the Earth and the moon. It really is a big deal."

Ionia turned and looked up, "Hey! Would it be pothible for you to get your telebot thingiesth to thsnag a little thpace duth for me?"

"Sorry Honey, no way! No freaking way."

Ionia bowed her head and pressed her temples. Her eyes filled with tears.

Jaa said, "Just kidding, Sweetie-Poops. Of course, I can get my little sweetie some space dust."

He swept her in his arms and squeezed her like a boa embracing a mouse.

Ionia's mind raced. She would create a line of super fabuloloso beauty products - better than those stinky French or Italian ones. She'd call it, "Space Station Face Cream Base." She pictured ads on the sides of balloon transport mobiles featuring her beautiful face with comets and moons orbiting her horn.

"I can't tell you how happy that would make me."

"None of this is public yet."

"My lipth are theeled."

"We've never had an opportunity like this before."

"Wow," said Ionia, the whites of her pretty eyes sparkling.

She loved Jaa. She really did. But lately she had to admit she'd been bored silly with his obsessing over stupid bacteria. She would cringe when he dragged his filthy little bugs into conversations at social gatherings; no matter how many times she told him to stuff a sock in it, Jaa just couldn't keep blabbering on and on about how bacteria, NOT GOD, built us humans billions of years ago out of algae or something.

After Jaa agreed to collect space dust for her, Ionia made a U-turn and became interested in the upcoming close encounter. After a few martini and Bopper cocktails, she'd even join the conversation if asteroids came up. And once, when Jaa hesitated for just a second, to search for just the right word, Ionia grabbed and ran away with the conversation, "Bacteria are very purpothful. They mutate like crazy - just for fun. And over millionth of yearth they built and perfected genetic archetypeth for, not juth us human beingth, but all creaturesth here on Earth."

Jaa quickly grabbed the conversation back, "It's my personal belief that these bacteria accomplished all this by altering their own DNA enabling them to grow whatever they needed, legs and wings, fins. Whatever."

But she butted in again, saying, "And there are literally billionsth of desthcendentsth of alien bacteria living inthide our bodiesth—on our thkin. Gueth how much bacteria the average human carrietths around! Go on, Guessth! Thirty poundsth! I'm not kidding!"

At twenty, Ionia still boasted wondrously pale skin, like a white dog's under-belly. Rich elite ladies the world over imitated her signature hairstyle. She'd had thousands of hairs implanted, which together with her natural straight locks, were professionally squeezed under tremendous pressure, then lacquered into a life-like rhinoceros' horn dyed battleship gray. An award-winning photograph featured her with her razor-thin arms draped over a robust naked hairy man whose arousal was in full view. She wore purple glitter lipstick over a realistic 3-D orange scorpion tattooed on her lower lip. Motion activated speakers seductively lisped, "Maybe I'll kith it. Maybe I'll bite it off. Dare to find out?"

***

The asteroids were to arrive just after sundown. That day Ionia cuddled close to Jaa on their Barca-lizard. She fluttered tiger eyelash implants against Jaa's neck as the AI Rubberhead on Belda TV discussed "Evening With The Asteroids." Jaa tried to pay attention to the tv while Ionia nibbled his ear.

From the day they first met, Jaa had always found Ionia irresistible. But lately, her voracious sexual cravings concerned him.

As Belda TV's Dr. Bernard Blaskellsky explained, "Fear of death and extermination may be stimulating women's vulvoidal glands to release an over-abundance of hormones urging them to make babies—while they still have time." Ionia was no exception. But fulfilling Ionia's needs had caused Jaa's right testicle to swell and throb like an impacted tooth. Gently he pushed her away.

"Not today, Love-Bunny."

Refusing to take no for an answer, Ionia gently nudged Jaa's purdilonimus with her horn until Jaa finally moaned and began caressing those famous vinylized breasts of hers, cooing, "Ouch. Jeeziz Baby, you're gonna kill me."

After their interlude they napped until dusk. Then, allowing enough time for three or four Hope Boppers to kick in, Jaa and Ionia emerged from their underwater bubble to launch their 33-foot balloon-boat, and head the short 25 yards to the White Street Platform to take advantage of what everyone agreed would be the best view of the Western sky over which the asteroids would come into view.

They tied up to their slot post at the base and rode the gondolavator sixty feet up to join the laughing crowd under a murky sky with a few purple thunderheads approaching from the North. For weeks, silver-tongued AI rubber-head spokesnorters for God, Jesus, the Devil Insurance Corporation, and even NPR, had flooded Belda TV with wild speculation.

"What do you think," asked the rubber-head called Hawk, "Will this be the end of days as foretold in the Book of Parable?"

The highly popular rubber-head called Teddy Bear-Mom answered through full lips, computer generated to radiate intelligence, "It just might. My daughter asked me if this asteroid close encounter might usher in the Age of Aquarius?"

"What did you tell her?"

"I told her to go ask her father. He thinks he knows everything."

Together they chuckled perfect horse-teeth at the camera.

As Jaa and Ionia walked along the tower deck, Jaa waved to a tightly clustered group dressed in black chain-mail vests. Fluorescent green elf-runes scrawled across their backs declared them members of The Brothers in Arms Doomsday League. Jaa only wore his vest to the bi-monthly meetings. Their girlfriends wore dermal goat masks.

"Wha-ho, Jaa-Boy!" they shouted, pawing the ground with hoof- boots equipped with shaggy fetlocks. Their ladies bleated like goats in estrus, "Aaannnnnnnnnnh! Aaannnnnnnnnnh!"

"What the Hell ith wrong with thothe women?" lisped Ionia, her pretty face twisted in revulsion, "I hope you don't find them attractive. Do you, Jaa? Tell me the truth."

"No way, Honey. You're the prettiest girl in the world."

Ionia didn't like Jaa's friends. She didn't like that he was a member of that club. She put up with them for his sake. She pulled Jaa away toward the end of the deck where they were scanned before being allowed across the velvet rope to join their rich neighbors scanning the horizon. Overhead, a full December Wolf Moon, plump and white, glowed.

All night, the brutal sky had been unleashing acid yellow electro-cord bolts that sizzled into the sea. With a loud hollow thunderclap, one hit perilously close to a cruise barge filled with intoxicated gawkers. One of the revelers aboard shouted to raucous laughter, "Rapture me up, Mofugger!"

A raspy woman slurred, "That all you got, Big Guy? You call yourself a Zeus? Come on, show us sumpin' real."

"I can't believe Jesuth-freakth are thtill carrying on with that rapture crap." snarked Ionia as another bolt flashed and struck the unruly cruise barge. There were screams as people jumped into the water. At that moment, Jaa's and Ionia's Hope Boppers kicked in.

Despite the victims' cries for help, the couple couldn't help feeling something good was going to happen, something wonderful. And when Jaa looked at Ionia's face in the purple evening light, he saw a face nearly as beautiful as the day they first met on the school bus long ago when love had been immediate and as crisp as their new J.C. Penny school clothes. Upon first hearing Ionia speak, Jaa had fallen under the spell of her childish lisp, the result of a fox tongue graft when she was just four years old. Although illegal now, it remains common practice for women to have their tongues bleached and tattooed with Elfin letters.

Ionia swore fidelity to Jaa back in the summer of 2009, the day they entered sixth grade, vowing to the moon goddess, Selena, she would love him forever. They were both idealists and swore abstinence until they turned fourteen. But raging hormones made them break their vows that same night.

Now, hand-in-hand, married and lovers forever, their minds bristled with expectancy. They marveled at the array of phosphorescent green plankton quivering in the sea below.

"I like to think thome day, just like thoth glowing sthea-cookumberth are communicating with the moon, I'll be able to talk with her too." said Ionia just as the first asteroid came into view above a storm-tattered American flag still waving bravely over the flooded Fort Zachery Taylor. From this distance, the asteroid called Baby Girl, in reality as large as Alabama, seemed a mere pelican in the sky. Seconds later the second and much larger asteroid called Moby-D appeared, flanked by two tiny pulsating lights.

"My telebots!" whispered Jaa, full of wonder at his own accomplishments in life; how this was just the beginning. What incredible discoveries and gifts DID the future hold for him and for all mankind?

Like Australian heelers chasing a car, the telebots wove in and around Moby-D.

"They're harvesting your particles from the dust tail." said Jaa, squeezing Ionia's tiny hand.

The two telebots fluttered like butterfly wings, reminding Ionia of the Monarch wings decorating Queen Elizabeth's 100th birthday cake before the Scottish "Abolish The Monarchy terrorist" called Lassie MacGrayrocks slammed the queen's face deep into the cake.

But the memory was cut short when one of the telebots began to pinwheel toward Moby-D. A tiny flash lit the night sky when the telebot collided with Moby-D, shoving it off course.

"What the hell?" murmured Jaa.

Moby-D, with the erratically flashing telebot embedded in its side, began tumbling end over end, and unlike Baby Girl, which had slid silently past the moon, Moby-D submerged into the Moon's gut like a boxer's body punch.

The Moon convulsed. She coughed exhaling gray dust. She struggled to maintain her composure, but her weak magnetic core would have none of it. Everyone the world over sighed as our glorious inspiration for so much poetry, beauty, and love on Earth broke asunder. Continent-size boulders of ancient lunar fundament plunged in slow motion toward Earth. White hot, these balls of death would splash into Earth's oceans within two hours of Moby-D's impact turning them instantly into scalding steam.

Sensing the last tidal pull, Lola-Brigita felt rage. She sang out in a low and powerful voice for all whales and sea creatures to come join her attempt to satisfy eons of anger at human abuse of the planet. Responding to her call, thousands of whales, squid, anything that lived in water, male and female, young and old, swam fast and hard to join Lola-Brigita and those already ramming the old oil rig until it tumbled into the sea casting every human on it to their fate among the sharks who waited below, smiling.

Dolphin

by Bernie Bleske

"Look," Keith said, pointing out to sea. Distantly, a pod of dolphin, bottlenose, the Flipper kind, rose and submerged in a smooth, almost-too-slow curve. "Look," Keith said again, and Ansen saw that they were all across the horizon. A barracuda flung itself out of the water and rocketed across like a skipped stone. A whole school of smaller fish, snapper likely, did the same. "Panic," Ansen said. "They flee the sonar." Just then, not fifty feet from the pier, six dolphin broke the surface.

"Holy shit," Keith said.

They were huge animals, the gray of old battleships and just as scarred. When Ansen still had the boat, on the rare day he'd taken it out, they'd seen dolphin just once. Under cloudless sky and in transparent water, they'd had that animal free spirit. Not now. These animals were all industry. Their breathing burst from their heads in spray like ancient venting machines. The smallest was nine feet long. At the pier the water was murky and gave only a grudging vision of dying seaweed. Farther out were quick little waves, and after the dolphin went under not even a shadow was revealed. The afternoon was breezy and dull.

Ansen unbuttoned his shirt, took it off, then sat at the concrete edge and removed his shoes and socks. "You're crazy," Keith told him, then drank again from the bottle.

"I always wanted to do this," Ansen said. He put his

keys and wallet in his shoes, and for a moment held back, thinking of Keith and his money and the keys to his house and cars. It wasn't trust that finally let him go, but abandonment.

The water was entirely unnatural in long pants. He walked forward until the bottom dropped away. In that time the dolphin never surfaced. He swam hard for what felt like minutes, likely seconds. When he stopped and came vertical his throat burned with salt. Those waves, so small from shore, heaved him up, dropped him down, caught the wind and broke in his face with deliberate malice.

Again, Ansen was alone. He turned, treading hard, pants resisting every kick. Looking down showed nothing but his own stark and old chest, his old lazy stomach like a white ball keeping him afloat. A shadow moved below his feet and Ansen kicked up so hard his nipples came out of the water, but he sank just as quickly and was left with the fading chill of a victim's terror. Dolphin, he reminded himself, not sharks. Dolphin, just as one came out of the water an arm's reach from his face.

"Jesus," he said. Then, "Hey there." The animal eyed him. It had a big eye, folded into gray flesh. Its blowhole opened and closed wetly.

Play, Ansen thought, reaching forward. Silently the dolphin rolled and vanished. For a moment the ocean spun then the waves hauled everything smooth. "Hey," Ansen said, to nothing, to the empty bobbing sea. "Hey, come play."

Something grabbed his calf. Through his sodden trousers he felt a row of small teeth nip his skin, then he was yanked down. His face went under, just long enough for a swallow of sea, and he came up coughing, spitting out the ocean. He gasped and was bumped in the ribs. They're playing with me, Ansen thought without a trace

Dolphin

of joy. Two dolphin rolled in perfect unison, thirty feet off. Another wave broke in his face, stinging his eyes, and it all got blurry. He blinked furiously. He had enough, and pressed hard back to the shore, half expecting all the while to be pulled under, pummeled into drowning.

Keith helped him up. "They have teeth," Ansen said. He used his shirt as an inadequate towel. Keys, wallet, still there.

"What'd you think?" Keith said. "They're wild. The ones you swim with are orphans. Broken."

"Well," he muttered, leaving unsaid his vague satisfaction at what he'd done.

"You gonna swim with dolphin," Keith said, "you might as well make it the free ones."

Ansen looked away at the concrete picnic tables where Keith's people had set up their day camps, with shirts, food, and filthy towels scattered territorially. Just looking at them made him feel oily.

"I got some friends over there," Keith said. "Wanna meet 'em?"

Ansen wiped his face with the tail of his shirt. In this state, wet pants, bare salty chest, feet already gathering dirt from the pier, he could look at home with those men. What the hell, he thought, I'm retired. What else have I got to do? He shrugged, which Keith apparently took for a yes, since he grinned and handed Ansen the bottle. Saltwater still filmed his throat, so what Ansen tasted was warm scotch and the sea.

Harbor for the Homeless

Key West

by Mia Shawn

So solvent in Simplicity,
your treasure-trove is Time.
Your gold and diamonds, Sun and Sea Synchronicity.
Still stabs of social shunning to forever find.

Poets pushing pedals.
Corporate Officers on carts.
Heat and Hunger are your medals.
Heaven for the Homeless holds your hearts.

The Red Gloves

by ML Condike

"Isn't that the homeless fellow we saw stumbling around at Truman Waterfront Park yesterday?" I said as my young college-aged friend Emily and I walked along Front Street toward the Custom House.

"Smells like it." Emily scrunched her face. "Guess he didn't get the free shower he'd hoped for."

The ragged-looking man lay sprawled on the steps of CVS at the corner of Front and Duval, sound asleep and wearing crimson red gloves. His once khaki, now grayish-brown shorts had slipped down letting his butt crack smile. His threadbare backpack served as a pillow and a half-empty beer cup sat one step up. Strings of greasy hair covered most of his face.

A policeman rounded the corner, walking with purpose. Simultaneously, I heard a *tap, tap, tap* on the CVS door. A face peered out the glass and gestured toward the vagrant.

The policeman nodded, approached, and patted the sleeping man's shoulder. "You can't sleep here Scrib."

Scrib stirred, sat up and looked around.

"We should move on," I whispered to Emily. "He's definitely in a bad way."

"Let's see what happens." She watched wide-eyed as the uncomfortable scene unfolded.

"Scrib, get up. How many times do I have to tell you? This is not a homeless shelter. It's a CVS." The officer attempted to lift the boorish man but ended up in a fracas. Arms and legs flew. The backpack rolled to the sidewalk, flipping open. A book fell at my feet. In the process, the vagrant's pants slid further south.

I collected the hardcover, holding it at my side until it was safe to return it to Scrib.

Emily covered her mouth, stifling a nervous laugh at the site of the man's bare backside.

Scrib gained his balance, pulled up his shorts, then waved his hands showing off his crimson red workman's gloves. "What about these?"

"What about them?" The officer's blank look matched my reaction.

"What next?" I mouthed to Emily.

She shrugged.

"These are magic gloves," Scrib bellowed. His proclamation caught the attention of a flock of tourists meandering by with their city maps flapping in the ocean breeze. As they hustled past with noses in the air, a woman uttered, "Disgusting."

"Officer Clark. I've got this. Let me take him." Another scruffy man had appeared from nowhere. His paint-covered smock hung below his shorts. He'd used the same barber as Scrib.

Relief washed over Officer Clark's face. "I know he's harmless, Vince. But he'd better find another place to flop. CVS is about to file a complaint."

"I'll keep my eye on him, Officer." Vince turned to his friend. "Come on pal. Let's go find some shade. It's gonna be a hot day."

"Just a minute," Scrib said and shook loose of his friend's grasp.

"What?" Vince reached but missed catching Scrib's arm.

Brow furrowed in deep concentration, Scrib rubbed his red-gloved hands together, then blew on them several times. Once convinced he was ready, he grabbed the half-filled beer cup and took a huge swig. His entire body shuddered, and his face contorted.

"The beer must be flat," Emily whispered.

I nodded a little surprised at such a strong reaction.

Scrib scratched his head as he perched the cup precariously on the edge of a CVS planter. "Why didn't' it work this time?"

"Why didn't what work?" Vince asked.

"The spell." He glanced at Vince, then lifted his hands to reexamine his red gloves. "Remember? They're enchanted. Last time I wore these gloves and drank piss, it turned to beer."

Vince rolled his eyes. "Cripes! They aren't magic gloves. You snatched my cup and drank my beer before I could stop you."

"You're sure they aren't magic gloves?"

"Positive." Vince's face softened. "Don't you remember our walkabout? Finding the gloves in The Home Depot lot?"

Scrib plopped onto the stairs, sniffed the remaining liquid in the cup and muttered, "Piss."

"Afraid so, Pal." Vince grimaced.

Scrib held his head in his hands and moaned, "I'm losing it. What've I become? This life's killing me."

Emily tapped my shoulder. "Mirror moment."

I looked at her. "What?"

My literary young friend pointed at the book in my hand.

I lifted it and read the title. "*The Hero with a Thousand Faces* by Joseph Campbell."

Emily picked up the tattered backpack, peeked inside and pulled out a spiral notebook. "It's full of these."

I placed 'Campbell' into the pack, took the notebook from Emily, opened to a random page and read a few paragraphs.

When I turned to answer Carver, a light flashed beside me. A sunray breached the clouds and entered his office window. It reflected off a lady's antique secretary stored in the corner amid a cluster of chairs, a trunk, and an old bookcase.

The desk reminded me of my office remodel at home. Sam and I had bought our Victorian house eight years ago. We started a room-by-room restoration beginning on the ground floor. Last year, we reached the second level, redid our bedroom, started on my office, then refocused on a nursery when I became pregnant.

Waves of sadness ebbed and flowed as I studied the piece. Charmed by its simplicity and character, the secretary attracted me—a perfect fit in my 1800s decor.

"Nice desk. May I?"

"Sure. Help yourself."

A trace of fish odor hung in the air as I waded into the afternoon light. Shifting a table aside, I stepped closer, then swept my hand along its front. When I touched the inlaid tulip on its hutch, it felt warm. Pigeonholes and tiny drawers with green knobs revealed themselves as I rolled back the top. A desire to possess the piece intoxicated me. "Is it for sale? I'm restoring my office. It's a perfect fit."

The Red Gloves

"I wonder if Scrib is short for Scribbler? He's a writer for sure," I said to Emily as I put the notebook back into the backpack and handed it to Scrib. "Here. You dropped this."

"Thanks," he said, not meeting my gaze. He held the pack against his chest like a baby.

We watched as Vince and Scrib turned and headed toward Mallory Square. Scrib removed the red gloves and shoved them in with his books.

Vince mumbled something I couldn't quite understand. Then I heard Scrib say, "I've got a feeling we're not in Kansas anymore."

"Dorothy's red shoes," Emily said.

I nodded, then sighed. "Another lost writer."

The Arrival

by Judi D. Winters

"Finish the f-ing book," exclaimed my prim and proper, teetotalling, Manhattanite momma, mustering the last of her signature language. She was in the active stages of dying. But that small fact didn't stop this ninety-seven-year-old educational powerhouse of a petite woman who never missed an election since "the year of the flood." Proudly affixing a stamp to the mail-in ballot, she cast her vote one last time in 2016.

Mom's straight-faced answers to imbecilic medical intake questions were classic, especially the singular ask, "Are you pregnant?"

"Yes, three in the oven." Then a wearied pause, "I am pregnant with new ideas."

The one-liners came fast and furious right up until the end. I would ask her, "Who am I?" She would say with a fading twinkle, "my mother, my sister, my daughter, *mein tochter.*" Within a week of the colorful proclamation, I lost my guardian angel, my first beta reader, who always prefaced her critiques with a tender deadpan, "Who wrote this?"

At the time, *The Book,* aka *Fish on a Leash, Reeling in the Backstory of the Most Extraordinary Theft in American Educational History,* had been a work in progress for a decade. *The Book,* a nonfiction, often took a back seat to the habitual interrupter—the novel of life. Retirements, surgeries, and adventures to far-flung

The Arrival

destinations derailed my writing. After seven years as a caregiver, it was time to grow up and morph from an only child into a solitary writer. I desperately needed a change of scenery, an escape from the borders of my four walls and faded furniture, a self-imposed writer's retreat.

But where? New York was in the numbing embrace of winter's night. Randomly, I threw scarlet darts at an imaginary wall map, targeting writer's havens. Oregon and Washington—too rainy. Montana and Iowa—too snowy. Maine—too cold. Mom adamantly refused to go to Florida, feeling it was the promised land where retirees went to die, even when relatives migrated *en masse* seeking relief from the family's genetic curse—arthritis. But her supernal presence boomed. Go South, young woman! Go South! Springtime in Cayo Hueso, aka Key West (the spit of land as far away from Florida proper), felt—just right!

My brain needed to decompress; the wilds of the Florida Keys awaited. Searching the web's blue screen for a long-term rental, two bedrooms, two baths, internet access, and a pool was a given. As a self-taught chef and baker, priority number one was a tall order: a gas stove on a two-by-four coral island. I found my wrecker's treasure twenty-four-and-a-half degrees north of the equator: steps away from starred restaurants and a pedal ride from downtown. But most importantly, a short walk to one of America's oldest synagogues (established in 1887). Upholding tradition and duty, I vowed to say *kaddish* (the mourners' prayer) every day for a year in honor of my momma.

My Long Island leave-taking was out of character; the old-school system of organization tumbled into a general listlessness. Everything came on board in twos. I haphazardly packed the unattainable basics: rare spices—cardamom and anise seed, imported jams and jellies, uniquely shaped international pasta. Canned tomatoes: pureed, crushed, diced, whole, and the usual paper good suspects, weighed down the double-lined brown bags and a dozen recycled Amazon multi-sized boxes. Even though the rent-by-the-month house came fully equipped, I never leave home without my hot pink carrying knife bag or mini grinder, the paraphernalia of any good chef. Given the number of shopping bags and cartons, I had become a bag lady traveling toward that refuge, a burden-free writer's solitude for thinking with intentionality.

The night before departure, a nor'easter hit Long Island. The rain pelted, the wind whipped around the garage, and squealed through the window and door sashes as I crammed clothing and bedding into every nook and cranny of the car's passenger compartment, helter-skelter. The trunk, reserved for the technical tools and trappings of writing *The Book* had to be methodically packed. Three clear plastic boxes contained ten years of amassed documents: thousands of hardcopy files—legal papers, newspaper articles, interviews, and topical research. Writing nonfiction is onerous. *The Book* is not an airport novel. It won't be found in a waiting area kiosk's rotating book rack.

The parting of the waters forced me to make a late 10:10 a.m. start. Believing the mapped route would speed me through the terrain of the Brooklyn reeds, I encountered a problem more serious than the bumper-to-bumper traffic. Mr. Acura GPS and Mz. Apple iPhone Waze continually disputed the routes. Even with my well-honed navigating skills, it was impossible to reconcile their coordinates. Mz. Waze almost always won out, her guidance system accurate and vividly exciting. "Car stopped, accident ahead, traffic jam, hazard, speed camera, police alert [poor police, they have lost the radar game], railroad crossing," and the weirdest alert for a New Yorker, "roadkill." This last directive would haunt me as I passed the Mason-Dixon line.

Riding solo left room for thought. Thinking aloud became a formalized art. Passersby presume you are talking on the cellie, allowing for audibly loud arguments in the absence of others. There are several activities a driver can engage in on a long haul: 1) jiggle and jive to blaring music, 2) do tight-quarter arm, leg, and ankle stretches—definitely no ab-gyrations, 3) meditate in the relative silence heard above the road thrum and compose lines for *The Book* that might bridge difficult passages. I became introspective: reviewing, redefining, and fleshing out the course of my life. A philosophical trinity. The Age of Adventure, the Age of Stability, and now the Age of Equanimity.

Pulling an all-nighter and driving 1571 miles non-stop to The End of America was not in my vocabulary. Preventing driver's fatigue, eyestrain, deep vein thrombosis, or stress was the impetus for scheduled friends and family pit stops. I not only needed to decompress, I needed to reconnect to the world of the living. The first overnight was in McClean, Virginia.

Rising early to beat the Washington D.C. traffic, I skipped the Edgar Allan Poe Museum in Richmond, VA (a literary sightseeing destination), and cruised at a sweet seventy, flowing into I-95's newly constructed E-Z Pass lane. The road parted like the Red Sea. I outran the Ford F-150s and souped-up Honda's when a WaveRunner started tailgating. No road rage. I just wished I had a kids' BB gun to aim at her tires. Oxymoronic for a pacifist. When the opportunity presented, I safely changed lanes. Accelerating, the driver demonstrated southern hospitality and gave me the finger in passing.

Judi D. Winters

I exited I-95 and headed diagonally towards Charleston, SC which like Key West welcomes ghostly visitors. Outside of Florence, I entered the low country. This appellation did not lose its import. Like the Netherlands, the water table is high enough to boot the trunks of trees.

These were not New York City's potholed roads. The undulating swampland mimicked Coney Island's famed roller coaster, the Cyclone. Zooming along desolate, well-paved roads through the hamlet of Laurel, churches cropped up at every bend. I counted nineteen. Pilgrim's Church caught my eye. I suspect if the Pilgrims had made it this far south, it would be to re-find their Dutch roots in the land that lies below the water table. In backwater Salters, I had a face-to-face with a massive steamroller. The smell of tar overshadowed the trees redolent with blossoming lilacs and the scent of cotton fields.

Departing Charleston, the state road took me through salt marshes populated by cord and *Spartina* grasses. A kettle of turkey vultures was circling above while a wake of vultures madly pecked at the roadside carrion. Mz. Waze failed to alert me to this nightmarish roadkill. A fifty-five-mph glance told me the object did not resemble the remains of an animal. Was it some homeless person wrapped in their sole possessions? Was I having a Hemingway-esque moment? Did I imbibe one too many the night before?

Returning to the mainland and I-95, I crossed the Tulifiny and Coosawhatchie Rivers just outside of Yemassee, when nature called. Fortunately, I had just entered Georgia. The visitor center loomed larger than life. Although this was a hurry-up call, I stopped to chat with an old friend seated on a bench about life's box of chocolates—a precast likeness of Forrest Gump was as still as a church mouse.

The last border blazed in the noonday sun. "Welcome to the Sunshine State." I passed Exit 333 (half the devil's sign), and three billboards in a row advertised the state's clairvoyant attorneys specializing in collisions. This section of road gave me the willies. Only six hundred and thirty more miles.

Flying low at 95 on 95, I switched to the Sawgrass Expressway. My well-balanced Bose speaker system played the essential Jimmy Buffet. The mood shattered as two highway signs bellowed, "Parkland! Parkland!" Thousands have probably driven by this suburban upscale Florida city, never noting the signs. Carrying my recent personal tragedy along for the ride was compounded by the surreal realization parents had lost children. Momma always said the loss of a child is beyond words. Momma knew, she had lost my brother before I came along. I can't imagine that grief. Like Mount Rushmore, Parkland, Paducah, Columbine, and Sandy Hook are blights etched forever on the American conscience.

At the end of mainland USA, a Homestead farmstand lured me from U.S. 1. I gathered two bushels of oranges and grapefruits for my daily fresh squeeze. Taking the Jewfish creek drawbridge, I headed to Key Largo. The name refers to the protected Australian Goliath grouper that nurses in tidal creek mangroves and barred from Floridian menus.

The two-lane 128-mile stretch of Overseas Highway suffered from sporadicity. Sometimes travel was fast, sometimes slow. Sometimes traffic was at a New York standstill; always a crapshoot on this one-way-in, one-way-out road. Surrounded by the North Atlantic Ocean and Gulf of Mexico waters, creatures and crossings

Judi D. Winters

blurred as I traversed the keys, the bridges, the channels and the creeks. Each bore a descriptive name: Cow, Big and Little Duck, Fat Deer, Pigeon, Snake, Shark, Racoon, No Name, and Tea Table, overpowering imagery for an overactive writer's mind. I chomped to get back to *The Book* and could smell the ocean air and taste the salt water as Mile Zero neared. Mom, I arrived intact at the seasonal rental to which I would return time and again, the Coral Frog.

During hurricane season, surging sea waters wash the Island. Trees and foliage, probably even some of the Islands' old salts, literally brine. Saltwater and trees do not play well together unless the trees are self-filtrating mangroves. They cannot evacuate. Eventually, the ashen gray eucalyptus returned to a glossy green. And the battered palms, orchid, frangipani, poinciana, and bougainvillea flowered. These natural splashes of color reflect the multicultural Human Face of America's Southernmost Point.

After setting up my dual-computer-desk niche, organizing my books, and docking my file boxes, I cloaked myself in the writing life and hit *The Book* running: up by 7:00 a.m. for a ten- mile circular bike ride to catch the shimmering sunrise. My daily ritual mirrored the Island's rhythm. After long hours of diligently and painstakingly unpacking and repacking *The Book's* data, especially the legal and financial facts and figures for a reading audience, I quit whenever the muse abandoned me, or a tourist parasailer invariably flies directly into a power line, pulling down the grid.

The story goes that Hemingway was up at 6:00 a.m., quit by 2:00 p.m., and headed to Captain Tony's on Greene Street. Following a legendary bout of fisticuffs, his party moved to Sloppy Joe's for their daily drinking meetup.

The Arrival

By June, temperatures reached well into the 90s, even with off-island breezes. I would grab my go-to libation: a glass of seltzer water. Practicing chewing bubbles became a fine art. Was it the intensity of writing or the proximity of the equatorial sun? I had moments of Hemingway-esque madness and heatstroke hallucinations, including visually sharp replays of the Conch Republic's toilet paper and day-old-Cuban-bread sea battles for independence.

Writing is not a predictable nine-to-five routine. Energized by the knowledge that *The Book* was on a steadily forward trajectory, it was time to party. Bicycling became my preferred mode of transportation, especially when pressed for time (retirees don't respond to the clock's dictates) to attend any of the myriad island-wide cultural events. Two topographical areas slow down a biker or a tipsy walker. First, the notorious Solares Hill, an eighteen-foot rise above sea level and a mile-high difference in barometric pressure, and the second, working the pedals on the steeply arched First Street Garrison Bight bridge. But neither deterred me from the allure of Duval Street. The weekend fairs, parades, theatre, songwriters and murder mystery festivals, poetry readings, and writers' conferences were Siren calls: day, night, and weekends.

The aromatic flora welcomed me in full bloom even if the fauna did not. Oxen-sized palmetto bugs and sugar ants confounded my daily existence. *Garumphing* cane toads, lime-colored-geckos, roosters who can't tell time, chirping iguanas, and rising waters were constant reminders renting was more desirable than homeownership.

I knew my time was drawing to a close, when I started conversing with an anole about its meal plan and pointed to the most truculent offerings. The anole, like the songbirds, became full-throated as the no-see-ums caught an odiferous sargasso breeze and flitted away. It was time to get "outta" Paradise and return to the reality of northern climes. Like momma, I am a born and bred New Yorker. Spending summer's *Caniculares* days on a sand beach drew me back to the city that never sleeps, to the One Human Family that opens ten million arms.

And like momma, a 1919 pandemic survivor, the Covid-19 pandemic had arrived and affected island living. Therefore, I decided to abbreviate the journey by miles and hours and board the Auto Train, where the tracks' cadence mimicked the contemplative progressions of my never-fully-at-rest writer's mind. After several seasons of coming and going, I have taken a temporary hiatus from the ritual drive north to south and back again.

Although the iconic Key West Welcome sign was in my rear window, and my 24"- wheeler with the purple, yellow, and white mottled cow horn across the rear seat replacing the consumed staples, I never really left the sprightly spirits of Key West behind. A bit of Key West zaniness pervades my surroundings. In a reclaimed upper-floor bedroom with the sun streaming through double-paned windows, I tell stories about and to the lithographs of Mr. Tortoise, Ms. Flamingo, and Mr. Pelican. I had the good fortune to make their acquaintance at a Marathon art gallery and enjoyed the pleasure of their company for the duration of the ride to NYC. Today, they reside on the walls of my writing studio, where I am tethered like a fish continuing to pen the Great American nonfiction. Yes, the writing is still ongoing and has entered its teenage years.

Momma, you wisely and compassionately taught me that patience is a virtue. But, momma, I hope yours

The Arrival

has not worn thin. I am sorry to report the "f-ing" book remains unfinished.

Spiral

by Josie Mintz

Sandy beach
   warm sun
      discarded
         unwanted
            unneeded
So close to where I began

Facade bakes
   spikes protect
      fragile
         pink
            interior
Aching for return to ocean's embrace

Drifting back
   remembering you
      tenderly
         reverently
            seductively
Delicate fingers caress hidden curves and depths

Spiral

Now cruel
    waves pound
        lurching
            chipped
                broken
Losing pieces of myself

Until finally
    even mercifully
        cradled
            released
                spiraling
Blissful return to ocean's womb

Resting place
    silent sway
        warm
            dark
              repose
Ending where I began

Naked and *Unafraid*

by Jennifer Juniper

My 50th birthday present to myself was moving to Key West. A veritable kick in the pants, leaving imprint: Are you going to actually *be* a writer or are you just gonna keep talking about it? I'd further reasoned (or maybe it was the tequila) if I can't become a writer in Key West—riding the creative wave of so many legends and finding support amongst all the aspiring contemporaries—well, then, I probably wasn't a writer after all.

Bouncing down Duval in a tutu, lit—the tutu, not me, not yet—lacy bra top, unicorn headband, and glow stick accessories toward a party promising five DJs. It was the second day of my first Fantasy Fest. Last night I was all agog, balancing the scads of scantily clad against the societal stigma of such wardrobe choices. I tried to suppress my conditioning, but it kept popping back up.

Nothing prepares you for Fantasy Fest. My hometown had a Freak Fest stretching the street from college to capitol, lined with pubs and a couple stages of rock bands. Open intoxicant laws suspended in the city crowned the Binge Drinking Capital of the World: Madison, Wisconsin. But we wore costumes. There were no butts showing, and men kept their junk tucked.

Shock had been my first reaction, and with it, before I could stop it, the word slut. Because that's what it means when you're almost bare, parading your wares in public. Doesn't it? You can't just push aside societal norms and all the puritanical programming that comes with having a vagina. Can you?

How can they do that? gave way to admiration for the creativity and courage it took. One woman in particular caught my eye, wearing nothing but paint depicting her as a severely short-shorted, shirt deeply unbuttoned, referee. Complete with a painted silver whistle dangling above her black and white striped naked navel. Her nipples *and* confidence protruding out as passersby stopped her, asking permission to snap a photo. I looked at her like she was a different species. And she wasn't alone. A tidal wave of people wearing nothing but painted-on designs flooded the street—a tiger, a mermaid, Daisy Duke—their skin a blank canvas for an artist who doesn't get to sign their work.

Seeing how little so many people wore had me feeling inspired the next evening. Changing back and forth between shorts and undies underneath the tutu, trying to dredge up courage and ultimately compromising on a pair of lacy boy shorts. It was definitely the least amount of clothes I'd ever worn in public, save for a bikini at the beach, and I felt a mixture of sexy self-consciousness. It was easy to be confident when you had a toned tight body. I had never fit into such a category and felt far from it now.

Afloat in a sea of skin, I almost bumped into a guy wearing only a puppy dog face painted across his groin. His penis painted pink for the tongue—which made it look like it wasn't painted at all. He could barely get three steps without someone stopping him in amazement to snap a pic. A small crowd swarmed him when he tried crossing the street, a "pupparazzi" if you will.

My emotional quotient was two parts admiration and one part agitation. *What does he have that I don't?* I wondered. A penis, sure, but seriously. What possesses all these people to put their practically naked selves out there and just stroll the street like it's no big deal?

I wish I could do that.

My hand fluttered to my exposed midriff. I felt a little overdressed. The whap of something hitting the backside of my knee startled me out of my reverie. Such a tender spot, stinging from impact, then soothed by the tickling soft fringe of leather. I pivoted back toward the source to see one of the few familiar faces on the island, now sporting a drawn-on black mustache.

"I thought I recognized those long, luscious legs!" Pat, now Zorro, with a black leather vest across his bare chest, held up the riding crop with a wicked smile spread across his face. We'd met as part of a singles group that mingled once a month for dinner or sometimes brunch. And while I hadn't made any love connections, I'd gained some fun friends—Pat was one of them.

I was glad to have his company, and his compliment. After a good-to-see-you hug, he fell into step beside me, tapping people gently from behind, on their behind, with his crop. Each one turned and smiled. Most acted turned on, hiking up a hip and asking for another. No one complained.

"Here," he passed his makeshift whip over to me, "I think you could get away with it better."

I was hesitant, but it's the festival of anything goes, so I gave it a try. I got even better reactions. Some asked for more. Many asked for harder. One asked for more and harder. Over and over and over again. Neither designed nor built for such avid activity, the prop disintegrated under the pressure. We had to pop into the Adam & Eve Lingerie & More store in search of a replacement. A proper one. And I was the one to try them on.

"Bend over!" Zorro's commands were not to be ignored.

This was far removed from any Halloween I'd ever celebrated. A real I-don't-think-we're-in-Kansas-anymore moment.

***

I had loved Wisconsin, but it was too cold. The winters were starting earlier, lasting longer, registering lower on the thermometer. Turning on the heat in June to take the chill out of the house, I saw my love had limits. I'd escaped the last few winters to warmer climes, making me more sensitive to cold, but also making me bolder. I longed to break out of my born-and-raised-in radius, lusted after the open road. Selling the house would be my impetus—I'd already be packed.

I was living on a launchpad.

Added bonus: finally breaking free of a six-year, on-again-off-again relationship, tortuous and passionate as only two Scorpios can make it. I wanted out—needed to end it, once and for all. My ovulation had gotten stuck in overdrive and was starting to override any logical decision making. It was like my ovaries were calling last call and my eggs had ordered shots. I wasn't safe alone with him. I wasn't safe out, either.

Jennifer Juniper

Rolling my cart down the pasta aisle debating red or white sauce, I spotted a man bending over to get a canned tuna off the bottom shelf, an effort clearly stressing the seams of his jeans. My mind dropped meal planning like a show gone to commercial, switching channels to a scene of me moving behind him. My finger hooking into the belt loop above one of those tightly clothed, tightly muscled butt cheeks, pulling him up until he's pressed against me, my suppleness nestled between the jagged hard edges of his shoulder blades while my other hand circles around his hot torso, hitting the cool metal of a button, then splaying my fingers across his fly, sliding them down the flap, a growing bulge filling into the hollowed-out palm of my ha—

I whipped my cart around mid-aisle, hands gripping tight lest they fly of their own volition and agenda. *I'll make something else for dinner.* Once outside, I moved quickly, intensifying the throbbing against the seam of my own jeans. Only when I was safe inside the car with the doors locked did I exhale.

At an appointment made the next day with my female nurse practitioner, I led with the craziest thing I was thinking. Figuring she'd shut me down, ease my mind, and we'd both have a good laugh. "I feel like I'm cycling twice a month."

She looked up from reviewing my vitals, straight faced. "Oh, you could absolutely be cycling twice a month."

"What fresh hell is this!?" Now, when my age makes the side effects of birth control pills too dangerous, Mother Nature's doubling down on her bet of me becoming a mother? "How do I protect myself?" The period tracker app I live and die by (okay, fuck or don't fuck by) is useless. "Unless they have a perimenopausal version..."

She shook her head.

Great. When my hormones should be hanging it up, they've decided to diversify.

***

The next morning, cleaning showers and scrubbing toilets at the campground I worked at, I got talking with a camper also new here and trying to find her place in all this. She was looking for people to paint, and I was searching for the confidence to be painted. Neither of us knew what to really expect. Our kindred, hippie gypsy souls clicked, and she made me a generous offer.

"My booth's by Caroline's. Stop by, I'll paint you for free." In answer to my look of shock she fortified her offering. "You're cleaning the bathroom I'm using, it's the least I can do."

On the outside, my head was nodding yes in enthusiasm. Inside, there's already a catalog of all the reasons why this could never happen: thighs too big, butt too big, boobs too small, stomach too flabby—ditto my self-esteem. But she'd left me with a lingering thirst for the courage to do it. I filed it in the back of my mind because a girl can dream.

That night's party theme was superheroes. I wore a Wonder Woman tutu, but I'd upped my game underneath, swapping out the boy shorts for a pair of perfectly matched electric blue silk panties and a deeper cleavage top. Still, I admired those more brazen than me—being the most brazen I'd ever been. I saw a man, wearing only a dangling sweat sock a la Red Hot Chili Peppers, weaving through the crowd with a woman wearing only stickers on her nipples and a thong. Their hair as white as the sock. Did self-confidence come with age?

While I got ready for the next night's Red Party at Fogarty's, the idea tugged at me some more. I wore my super short, careful-not-to-bend-over-too-far shiny devil dress and hoped my red horns and I were moving closer to getting painted as we marched closer to the end of Fantasy Fest.

It was the last night, and true to form, I was getting it in at the last minute. On a Saturday night, tucked underneath the low branches of the banyan tree, I slowly slithered out of my clothes inside a white tent with zipped on walls. I was sure about the Poison Ivy design, but that's about all I was sure about. (I wish I could say the mantra getting me through was something along the lines of "I am woman, hear me roar," but it was more of a, "Nobody knows me here, nobody knows me here." Being new to the island, this was as undercover without any cover as I was ever going to get.)

Getting sketched and brushed so meticulously, watching artistic vision become reality on my body—I was both model and canvas. *Look at me being all bold and shameless.* If I'd known how radically empowering it would feel, I would've come sooner.

Skin turned green, personality transformed along with my body, the time came to step out of the safe little bubble. As I faced the outer world, a surge of self-deprecation seized me, squeezing my chest. I took a deep breath and held it, trying to break its grip and still all the fluttering inside. My knees were trembling so much, I looked down to see if it was noticeable. It was.

I entertained the idea of turning back, asking if I could watch the parade here, with her. Where it was safe. Where it felt so normal just seconds ago. Snapshots lining the walls with all those who had come before me, cheering me on. There, I was part of a tribe. Here, steadying my green villainous self on the top step, and balancing the courageous move I'd made with the self-image questioning it, I felt like a lone ranger.

But going back wasn't an option. When I turned to look into the tent, there was already someone else in my place, describing what they wanted. Even more so, I couldn't go back because then it would all have been wasted. Not the money or the paint or the time, but the reason why I wanted to do it in the first place, the reason it took me all week to get there—the bravery to join the unafraid, the unlimited, the omni-comfortable within their own skin.

This was my initiation.

I stepped out from the safe cocoon of the artist's tent into a world with nothing between us but colored skin. The first person asking to take my picture, three uncertain steps in, probably saw a confident woman. But what I was, was someone bargaining with herself. *Just make it to the crosswalk. Then sneak through side streets, jump on your bike and ride home. No one will know.*

Except me. *I'll know.* And I would carry with me how I bailed on myself and my high reach attempt—past the incessant self-conscious pitter patter of *I don't look good enough to be parading around like this*—to the top shelf with the good stuff: admiration of my own, unique beauty.

Screw that. I took a few more steps. And a few more people took pictures while saying, "Wow," and telling me how beautiful I looked. One guy was FaceTiming with his family in the Philippines. Another, sharing with his friends back home in New York. Their big smiles were making me smile. Their wide eyes conveyed they were impressed, and grateful for what I added to their entertainment, enhancing their experience—or something like that.

With every step I felt a little bit sexier.

I was on the other side of the wide eyes now, feeling powerful. I still felt self-conscious, but I kept putting one foot in front of the other until that feeling faded away, replaced by some little flicker of fame glowing inside from images of me traveling around the world. The looks on people's faces only seemed to fan the flame, not threaten to douse it as I had feared. It was the same for me as it was for anyone else who dared—we were applauded, smiled at with mad respect.

As the parade came to an end, beats from a DJ began wafting down from on high and I let them pull me to their source: a cool looking blonde in a captain's hat, spinning records, with lasers shooting out from behind her, swooping down and illuminating the crowd. It was music to lose yourself in. My hips writhed to her rhythms, my brain relaxed and relived the risk taken and the rewards received. Being naked in public was incredibly freeing. Washing away all trepidation, leaving only self-possession in its wake.

Naked and *Unafraid*

The lasers lit up a threesome and I tried to figure out which girl the guy belonged to and which one got folded into the mix like chocolate chips—a flavor enhancer but not a main ingredient. The confidence and the costumes we all were using to express ourselves, stirred a communal alchemy amongst strangers, making us less like strangers.

In turning toward the bar to take a quenching sip from my beer, a good-looking guy leaning against the wall caught my eye. Tall, dark, and cute. Wearing a long, dark, and fitted coat with a ruffled shirt peeking out. A smile sat on his face and a colonial hat sat atop a hair wrap.

I smiled and said, "Hey."

He "Heys," and smiled back.

The next song was a remix of something by Jay-Z I liked.

"Dance with me." I wasn't asking.

He pushed off with the foot resting against the wall and fell towards me in sexy dismount. We merged onto the crowded dance floor. When the song changed, I waved him away.

"We're done dancing now," back to a single I twirled, absorbed into the throng of tutus, capes, glitter, paint, and wigs.

He danced backward from me, back to his wall, and the crowd collapsed the space between us.

At one with the sticky mass of bodies, pulsing with this newfound command over myself and my life, I let the music penetrate until the bass and my heartbeat synced up, making me more wave than particle. I'm not looking for any attachments, I remind myself, I've just broken free of one. But such easy come, easy go-ness between us had me initiating contact once again.

"You should've dressed as Prince, and I could've been Apollonia!" I said. I touched his ruffled shirt as he leaned in close to hear. It had only been my dream Halloween costume since I was fifteen, when the movie *Purple Rain* came out. I figured him too young to get the reference.

"I was," he shouted back. "Yesterday," answering the surprise in my eyes with a SnapChat video to prove it.

The serendipity of it all was turning me on. A warmth began to spread inside me, making me turn the flirt up; touching his arm, looking longer into his eyes, pressing my cheek into his as our words competed with the music.

He snapped a selfie, and we danced some more. I asked his name.

"It's JJ."

"*I'm* JJ!"

Each of these things clicking into place between us became a light flickering on the path materializing before us. I'd always trusted anything which lined up easily—gifts from a Universe conspiring for my happiness. Then came that feeling. The flutter behind my belly button slowly snaking its way south, where it became a tingle—my body telling me I was going to sleep with him. A dizzying realization swirling my mind for a moment. I fixed my gaze on the dance floor, steadying myself while the cards in my deck shuffled.

Pressing my cheek back into his, lips moving against the curves of his outer ear, I made my move, "I'm going to the bathroom. When I come back, let's leave."

Naked and *Unafraid*

Checkmate.

"Okay," he pressed back, breath burning hot in my ear. "But if you don't come back, I'm going across the street for a sandwich."

The cuteness factor this added to his boyish face spread a smile across mine. I felt the heat of his gaze watching me walk away.

Once in the tiny quiet room, the sound and excitement muffles. Face to face with myself, I did a quick scan. *Am I being true to myself? Or just swept up in this free-for-all frenzy? Is this really what I want?*

A throb answered.

He stood in the same spot and we smiled knowingly at each other as I approached him. That's where the foreplay really began; both of us knowing what's was about to go down and every move made was an advancement toward it. Walking behind me down the stairs, he tipped his torso to the side, displaying his enjoyment in watching me descend, like a gourmet buffet he's contemplating where to begin eating first. In his culture, my thighs aren't chubby—they're thick. A sought-after size.

We moved from our chance meeting, stepping out into the world together, a transition dripping with anticipation. What would we do to each other and whose bed would we do it in?

Between bites of sandwiches we talked logistics. Deciding his place instead of mine and negotiating the size of his trunk and the likelihood of my bicycle fitting inside. I was skeptical. It had a big basket decorated with skulls and chains from last week's zombie ride. But he got it in. (A little piece cracked off the basket would remind me of this night).

My mind flashed back to the morning when I opened my camper door to a new, still-in-the-wrapper condom lying in the grass at the bottom of the stairs. I'd joked, maybe Key West had a condom fairy, promoting safe sex during this time of heightened promiscuity—kind of like the tax holiday encouraging preparedness at the beginning of hurricane season. Now I wondered if it had been a sign.

It had rained while we were dancing inside. I rescued my clothes, wringing them out to release some of the wetness.

And his, "Want me to pop 'em in the dryer?" while pulling into his driveway released some of mine. This was a new kind of turn on. A guy's willingness to do my laundry sparked the live wires of my sensuality.

In the center of his room, his bed glowed luminous in all its purity. White blanket, white pillowcases, white sheets. Hesitant and unsure, I looked down at the painted vines wrapping my legs.

Throwing off the covers, he invited me in with a husky, "Let's make a mess."

He kissed me, gently. Respectfully. Signaling his intent not to ravish and devour me—not right away—but to slowly savor. As he pulled away, I searched his eyes and scanned his place, gathering information on the lover I'm about to have. His big, easy smile said he took life in stride. The scrubs resting on the back of a chair testified to something in the medical field. He was tidy. And ironed. I took a deep breath; it quivered into my chest.

Naked and *Unafraid*

He slipped in, between the sheets and beside me—a stretched out cello. Stroking my curves, tracing my designs, admiring the craftsmanship. My skin buzzed with electricity and my insides liquified. His long fingers slid the strings of my center, thumbing the in and out of my hip bone. Lips leaving mine, trailing down the soft underside of my chin, my neck, to my jutting clavicle. Opening at my breast, drawing me into his mouth. His fingers rubbed an erect nipple between them, fine tuning, then nibbling to set.

My back arched, smooshing my red wig into the feather pillow cradling it. Hips and lips found rhythm while we touched and licked and squeezed and kissed. He had the eager, boundless energy of youth, making me doubt I'd get much sleep. Caressing the crease between my pelvis and thigh, a finger strayed to graze the place he wants to go next. Curves and strings, strings then curves, he played me until his palm anchored on my pubis and he started strumming. Ever so softly at first, it was still enough to ripple vibrations through my entire being. He had awakened me.

The kisses deeper, our touches stronger, the pace grew frantic, speeding to get where we were trying to go. We delighted in moving from the beheld to the beholder and from the prone to the predatory. The hardness of his longing pressed against me, begging me to open. Pulsing, it knocked, trying to patiently await invitation to my innermost room.

I clicked my buckle in for the ride he's operating, lifting me high, then swooshing me down the other side. Intertwined and smearing like an Andes creme de menthe candy twisted up in ecstasy. On the final crest we spasmed in tandem, our passion erupting...cascading. We were weightless.

We lay there panting, in our five shades of green. You can really let yourself go with someone you don't really know. Sex with a stranger offers sacred anonymity. Free of backstory and weighted expectations for the future, you have only now. Only this carnal pleasure. And you can be whoever you want to be within its immediacy. It's poetic.

The softness of a woman's body melding with the hard strength of a man's was a symphony I never tired of hearing. I hope someone is kissing my neck until my dying breath.

He brought me home fully satisfied and late for work. No numbers were exchanged. All I had were erotic echoes vibrating off my inner walls.

Good Luck

by Katrina Nichols

Tina's screams shattered the stillness of the hotel grounds and sent the pool boy running for the garden area. It was April in Key West, and the weather was hot already. I was cooling off in the hotel pool where had I met Tina earlier in the week. She was traveling with her husband to celebrate their 45th wedding anniversary, but he spent most of the week sport fishing. I was in Key West on a work assignment to write a feature article about day trips in Florida. We often chatted as we swam. I was young enough to be her daughter, but we found lots to talk about.

Now I watched from the deep end of the pool, horrified and amused as my new friend came stumbling out of the hotel's lush garden toward the pool area. Her shoulder was covered in what looked like brown yogurt.

"My God, what happened to you?" I asked.

But Tina was too upset to speak. She was busy pulling the sleeve of her t-shirt away from her neck. The pool boy came to her aid and led her to the poolside shower.

"It's OK, Miss Tina. Those nasty iguanas poop on all our favorite guests. It's good luck!"

He handed her a towel and she used it to swat at him, and hurled curses at him and the iguana both. I watched as he backed away and retreated in the direction of the hotel office.

Tina grabbed the pull chain for the shower, and the spray hit her full in the face. I went underwater to stop laughing but could still hear her muttering and cursing.

As petite as she was, Tina was loud when she was mad. I knew she was in her 70s, but she wouldn't reveal her true age. She was still standing under the shower when I came up for air. Her hair was plastered to her head and mascara ran down her face. Her t-shirt and shorts were soaked. She stood dripping wet and still mad as hell.

"Tina, let me help," I offered.

I got out of the pool and went to her, but she glared at me and stormed off to her room. Her sneakers *squish-squashed* as she went.

"Well, it's not my fault you got shit on!" I yelled after her. "He's right! It's good luck!"

But she was gone.

An hour later she was back. I was lounging comfortably and reading a book. She had changed into fresh clothes and looked like she was ready for a night out. I admired her ability to bounce back so quickly. She looked great. Her short brown curls were freshly washed and framed her face. She wore a white off-the-shoulder blouse with her black crop pants with a red belt for a splash of color. She looked terrific, I thought, and no one would ever know she had been upset just an hour ago.

"Let's go to dinner. I'm starving," she announced.

I shook my head and thought to myself: So that's how she will play it. Like nothing happened.

Good Luck

I lowered my sunglasses and looked at her over the top of my book.

"Where?" I asked.

"That restaurant down the block with the good antipasto. The one we went to for lunch on Sunday," she said.

"Bella Mermaid?"

"Yes," she said. "That's the one."

"Fine, let me change."

I went to my room and put on a comfortable sundress that fell just above my knees. I checked the full-length mirror behind the bathroom door and noticed the tropical sun had added some pink to my nose and shoulders. The light seafoam green of the sundress set off my dark green eyes. All I needed was a bit of mascara and lip gloss and I was ready.

Tina waited for me by the pool. We linked arms and headed for the street, like two school chums leaving campus. We hadn't gone ten feet when Tina stopped abruptly and pointed up. I followed her gaze to the tree line that bordered the edge of the hotel property and saw, perched on the widest branch of the tallest tree, a three-foot-long iguana staring down at us.

Tina shook her fist at it and screamed, "You beetch, you beetch, you poop on me, eh? I shoot you! I shoot you with a gun I find! I keel you dead, you beetch! You never poop on me again! I fix you!"

The iguana blinked once and moved further up the tree.

I dragged Tina further down the sidewalk and kept her moving toward the restaurant. She was shaking with fury and continued to look over her shoulder toward the tree that held her nemesis.

Once we reached the restaurant and went inside, I ordered dry Martinis. Tina still looked mad, and I hoped a cold cocktail would settle her down.

The waiter came and recited the menu specials for us. I ordered the shrimp scampi and Tina ordered the roast chicken. She looked smug now, but I couldn't imagine why.

"Tina, why did you order the chicken? You know their seafood is the best."

"I ordered the chicken because I have been told, the iguana, he is chicken of the tree."

We laughed and sipped our Martinis. I smiled at Tina now and wondered what the iguana was doing. Did he or she (as Tina assumed) even care that it nearly spoiled someone's vacation?

Tina caught my drift and raised her forkful of chicken in a toast. "To that beetch. If I ever catch her, I will fry her up and eat her!"

Then she popped the chicken in her mouth and savored the tasty morsel with closed eyes and a smug smile.

The Historian's Apprentice

by Amber Nolan

FADE IN

INT. OFFICE – DAY

A frumpy woman, the Key West HISTORIAN, enters a cluttered office carrying a mug. She goes directly to a shelf and pulls out a bottle of Jameson, pours it in the coffee and turns toward her desk, bottle in hand. She does not notice the professionally dressed young man, waiting in the client seat.

A SIGN on the wall reads "Never let the truth interfere with a good story." She sits behind the desk and sets the bottle down. She sips from the mug then LEAPS from her seat—extremely startled at the person seated across from her.

But her concern is the ALCOHOL LACED COFFEE— which she manages to save, catching one of the drops in her open palm.

                    HISTORIAN
        Who are you and why are you in my office?

                    YOUNG MAN
        Linda at the front desk sent me back here. I
        had an interview scheduled for 3pm. For
        the historian's apprenticeship.

> HISTORIAN
> And it's 3pm now. Strike one. I never trust anyone who is on time. And again, who are you?

> YOUNG MAN
> Nedward Ashbluff.

The historian holds up a hand.

> HISTORIAN
> I'm going to stop you right there. Your parents called you Nedward?

> NEDWARD
> They couldn't decide between Edward or

Ned.

> HISTORIAN
> What's your middle name?

> NEDWARD
> Hank.

> HISTORIAN
> You must hate them.

> NEDWARD
> I do ma'am.
> (beat)
> Is that whiskey?

He indicates the bottle in her hand.

The Historian's Apprentice

                    HISTORIAN
No, of course not!
          (beat)
It's Irish Whiskey. TGIF. Why did Linda
schedule an interview on a Friday?

                    NEDWARD
It's Tuesday, ma'am.

                    HISTORIAN
Do you want this job or not?

                    NEDWARD
Very much, ma'am. I love history. It's
always been my dream to record it.
          (beat)
I brought my resume...

Nedward takes it out of a portfolio to hand to the
historian. He seems nervous doing so, but the historian
ignores him, leans back, puts her feet up on the desk
and takes a drink.

                    NEDWARD
OK, just the highlights then. I was president
of the history club at my college, I helped
lead a monumental archaeological dig...

                    HISTORIAN
          (interrupts)
Nedward, here's the deal. I've been the
Florida Keys historian for 30 years, but this
new board has their head up their ass and is
trying to push me into retirement. They
want fresh blood. When I do retire, I want

someone who will keep things running my
way, not their way.

NEDWARD
What's their way?

HISTORIAN
The wrong way! They're all too concerned
with facts and accuracy. Do you have
experience, Nedward?

NEDWARD
As it says on my resume here, I have a
bachelor's degree in historic preservation,
and...

He attempts once again to hand the paper to the
historian, who waves him off.

HISTORIAN
(interrupts)
Pfff! Overpriced paper! Have you ever
actually recorded history?

NEDWARD
The ad said you'd train the right
candidate...

HISTORIAN
Ah, the newspaper. Boring! I considered
hiding golden tickets in Key Lime pies, but
that's been done already.

NEDWARD
I'm allergic to limes anyway.

The Historian's Apprentice

              HISTORIAN
Ah. Lymes disease. Brutal. So, I'm going to recall an important story. And YOU are going to write it down. Don't be afraid to spice it up—that's how I do things. Makes the official history more interesting.

There's an awkward beat.

              NEDWARD
I'm ready when you are.

              HISTORIAN
Back in the days before Jimmy Buffet lost his shaker of salt...

              NEDWARD
When was that, exactly?

              HISTORIAN
It doesn't matter, Nedward, but let's go with 20, 30 years ago.

              NEDWARD
Ok, got it.

Nedward writes on his paper.

              HISTORIAN
A long time ago, Key West was still part of Cuba...

Nedward stops writing and looks up, puzzled.

Amber Nolan

NEDWARD
Key West was never. Well, maybe Pangea,
but that was ancient times.

HISTORIAN
Are you going to keep interrupting?

NEDWARD
I apologize.

HISTORIAN
A circus carnie named Ponce de Lion was
searching for the fountain of youth. But he
discovered a mysterious force here, more
powerful than gravity.

Nedward reacts to her inaccurate pronunciation of
Ponce de Leon, but goes with it, smirks, and keeps
writing.

NEDWARD
Can you spell Ponce de Lion for me?

HISTORIAN
I talk, you record. Details are added later
when you type this into official records. But
that's if—and only if—I decide to hire you.
Right now it's not looking so good.

NEDWARD
I'll do better. Please, go on.

The historian takes another swig as Nedward flips a
page.

The Historian's Apprentice

> HISTORIAN
> Shortly after reaching our island, Ponce de Lion gave up his quest. He said the warm ocean waters were "close enough" to his forever fountain. Next page, Nedward.

She lights a cigar. Nedward sighs and flips a page.

> HISTORIAN
> In the 1800s, Blackbear the pirate navigated these waters. You've seen the movie, right? With Johnny Depp? I'm a sucker for that rebel-pirate look.

She's smiling and daydreaming at a fond memory.

> HISTORIAN
> Anyway, when Blackbear reached the Keys, the mysterious force struck again. He instantly lost motivation and purpose. So he retired and switched from piracy to do-goodery.

> NEDWARD
> Is do-goodery even a word?

> HISTORIAN
> As a general rule, Florida Keys historians can make up words as they see fit. Can I continue?

Nedward throws the pen down and tosses his hands up.

> NEDWARD
> Sure, go for it.

HISTORIAN
Later, a bunch of army guys tried building a
railroad bridge, but they too fell victim to
the mysterious phenomenon that forced
them to go fishing every day. So the bridge
was never completed.

Nedward is folding his resume into a paper airplane.

NEDWARD
(mutters)
Pretty sure a hurricane was involved, but
whatever.

He eyes a pile of dirty drink glasses on the desk. He
takes one, blows dust out, and pours himself a drink.
His tense, professional attitude is gone.

HISTORIAN
(clears throat)
Since then, scientists have come to Key
West to study the phenomenon, and
concluded it was a time warp. Those
findings were never published, of course.
But today it's known as "island time." So,
Nedward, moment of truth: read to me
what you have.

Nedward closes his notebook and pours some whiskey
in the historian's coffee mug.

NEDWARD
(while pouring)
Alright, look, I'm gonna level with you.

The Historian's Apprentice

He slouches down in his chair: it's time for serious talk now.

> NEDWARD
> I don't have a degree in anything. And I don't have Lymes disease. I'm a descendant of Tiki John.

> HISTORIAN
> The legendary bartender who invented the Rum Runner?

> NEDWARD
> Yes, that Tiki John. His recipe was stolen so I came here to find which bar took it—by tasting their drinks. But I had too many, accidentally borrowed a boat and ran it aground. I thought an apprentice job would look good for the judge.

> HISTORIAN
> Is all of that true?

Nedward swishes the drink around, confident now.

> NEDWARD
> Does it really matter?

Nedward gestures to her sign. The historian thinks for a beat, slaps the desk, leaps up, and raises her mug, spilling her whiskey a little.

HISTORIAN
Finally! Someone who gets it! Welcome aboard, Nedward.

They tap glasses.

HISTORIAN
Can I call you Hank?

FADE OUT.

"Oh no, not again"

by Earl Smith

Redundancy, relentlessly recurring,
    echoes through all the ages.
        Scenes, rehearsed billions of years before
        and lightyears away,
            a recidivating dance unendingly
            rehearsed and reprised.

~~~~~~~~~~

Redundant rhythms reverberate
    the restlessness of a stale Key West evening,
        replete with chattering clichés
        and crudely crafted woundings.
            The band grinds out counterfeit concoctions
            in approximated synchronicity.

An adolescently maladjusted Apollo advances,
    exuding pharmaceutically boosted masculinity.
    The damsel Daphne,
        nursing a not-drink drink,
            awaits,
                pondering the recurrent thought
                of the bowl of petunias,
                "Oh no, not again"

Earl Smith

The bartender, caressing a relatively clean glass
  with a not-so-relatively-clean rag,
    and reflecting on the senselessness
     of mind-dulling repetition,
      settles into a remembering
       rancid with regret and remorse.

~~~~~~~~~~

Fools they be. Fate's lieutenants,
  acting under an idiot's orders.
   But which Ahab and which
   the White Whale?

~~~~~~~~~~

He snipped and chemically rigged. She barren and
  pharmaceutically sedated.
   Ardent but uninspired, desire purposefully
    misinterprets diffidence as surrender.
     Resignation's daughter struggles to make sense
    of carnal brutishness.
     Needs, artificially almighty, disannul
     prudence eroded by tedium.
      The forever dance of denouement
      dominates the drama.

~~~~~~~~~~

"Oh no, not again"

In such places,
    lost souls wander well-worn warrens of self-indulgence,
        aching for the feeling of warm skin on skin
           and the quickened breath of another,
              yearning to resurrect the lie
                  that they are no more or less defiled,
                and, in cynical circumvention,
                    offering to distract, however briefly,
                      from the obvious and inevitable.

The Spanish instrument falls silent,
    relieved that its once sweet, sensuous voice,
        strangled through an electronic obscenity,
           and mauled by overeager ineptitude
              is, for a brief respite,
                mercifully stilled.

The anti-rhythmic barbarian, after asymmetrically abusing
    the most sacred instrument of the human heart,
        heads for the head to evacuate, with relief,
           the only truly impactful outcome of the evening,
              which contains a mutated strain of bacteria
              which will spawn a provincial,
                but persistent,
                mini plague of
                  Conch Republic diarrhea.

~~~~~~~~~~

Earl Smith

The evening, the place, and all the players
  are merely figments of a demented envisioning,
    empowered by disinterested inevitability.
      The ocean of time rolls insensibly on,
        mauling all it swallows.
          The denizens dance their distracted dances
          within its maw,
            never experiencing the warmth of the
            distancing sun.

Denying both myth and reality,
  Daphne cannot turn herself into a laurel tree,
    Apollo's ardent adulation will abruptly dissipate.
      Cupid's arrows, leaden or otherwise,
        will pass into memories never to be revisited.
      The bowl of petunias will mutter anew,
      "Oh no, not again"

~~~~~~~~~~

A night, a day, a week, a month,
  what are these in the great swing of time
    through the charnels of chaos?
    Eternally repeated dramas
      set in recurringly mindless absurdity.
    Each always tangoes alone.
      Passing whisps of dry, dying air.

~~~~~~~~~~

"Oh no, not again"

It is completed. She sits unnoticed.
  Closes her notebook, sighs,
      and wonders why she has more compassion for them
          than they seem to have for themselves.
              Trading scraps of their humanity
                  for delusion's brief respites,
                      ennui makes desperate fools of them all.

There is nothing more on this her final evening.
  It is time to depart this boneyard of humanity.
      The island, the bar, the figments
          will soon be forgotten.
              Another world, somewhere beyond Antares,
                  awaits.
                      Perhaps this next one will be different.
                      She has her doubts.

Pauline Pfeiffer Hemingway

by Elia Chepaitis

There never was a question
Of playing second fiddle.
If you were Fiddle
I'd be Banjo,
Even if it killed me.
Nor was I inclined
To play Dulcinea
To your Quixote,
And that was wise.
For I have noticed
That in the garden of your dreams,
I am included
Among the statuary

Love & Erections 90 Nautical Miles from Cuba

by D.E. Triplett

I was horny—like Key West horny. Barely sixteen, with the umbilical cord of my just-birthed driving privileges cut yesterday by a surprisingly sharp-edged learner's permit, I was a virile virgin practicing an unholy forced celibacy which would, I was sure, accompany a childless me to my lonely grave.

And I was in love—totally, madly, and sadly, unequivocally one-sidedly.

Studying at our kitchen table, trigonometry scrambling my brain as if the subset of geometry concerning triangles was a greasy cook at IHOP, I was thanking the postcard, realty seductive with the fortyish blonde agent smiling hungrily from it, for my latest untimely penile tumescence, when the cherished cuckoo clock behind me slurped the six o'clock hour. An heirloom passed down generationally, Mom protected the lewd chalet with a passionate fervor which meant, even with the poor little bird having only one eye and twelve feathers at last count, that it would stay up on the wall in pornographic perpetuity.

A whiplash kind of girl, my muse's name was Billie Jean Wade, and she was a senior like my sister, Sarah.

Sleek, hip, smelling like vinyl records and soul food, she rocked a wonderfully belligerent afro as she'd jazz down our high school's hallways knowing everyone it seemed. Invisibly, I sat behind her in Spanish II. And had I yet brewed up enough morning courage to tap a glossy shoulder and convey a simple *buenos* días to her, you ask? No, *yo era una gran gallina.*

Wondering how I'd even be able to enter her chic orbit to say anything without passing out, the cuckoo, shakily, finally retreated behind its double alpine doors. My stiffy, however, especially with Billie Jean now rocking my libidinous mind, didn't retreat at all; it was still charging forward like some kind of bold boner brigade. And as I began the gross attempt to dismantle it—by thinking of Grandad eating cottage cheese without his dentures—Randy burst in through the back door.

"I need a toad or frog, Percy, stat."

"Are you wearing a pair of Spider Kinos?" Asking, I was staring at the slim soles and straight stitching around the foot bed, the cartoonish-looking hand of the top strap whose fingers, brown and leathery, were gripping him between his small and remarkably tanned toes.

"Maybe," he said, turning his face and squinting at me.

"You do know those particular sandals are made for women?"

"It was just a footwear-complicated morning. Besides," he said, raising his hands with palms up. "We're on The Rock, man. Everything's fluid down here."

"Valid point."

"So do you got a toad or frog somewhere I can borrow? Maybe up in your room?"

Red-headed with twitchy eyes and a grifter's haywire moral compass, already the stuff of delinquent legend at twelve years old, little brother had single-handedly given our entire local school system a severe case of educational pedophobia. So, to say I was wary of loaning that prepubescent terror any kind of animal, even a handful of those little no-see-um bastards, was a fauna-concerned understatement.

"Why would I have a toad or frog up in my room, Randy?"

"I don't know," he said, wiping sweat from his freckled face with a forearm. "Thought you had something like that once."

"That was an ant farm."

"Oh, yeah, Jonestown."

"That was Mom's heartless name for it afterwards," I said, heatedly. "And I didn't cause a mass insectile suicide by the way. No matter what she says."

"Whatever, Jim Jones. Look, I can't bounce a frog higher off the ground than the Devlin twins if I don't have one."

"That's wrong on so many different levels. Do you really want to check off the last indicator of the Macdonald Triad, Randy?" A bed wetter and innovative arsonist, our family had started a pool as to not if, but at what age he'd become an official serial killer.

"Do you have a frog or toad or not, Percy? Or maybe even a newt would work. I'm not a hundred percent sure on the amphibious rules of this thing."

"Goodbye, Randy."

"Goddamnit!" As he flew out the door, I wasn't sure how far he'd get, since an ugly storm, beyond the short hedge of sea grapes in our napkin-sized backyard, was spreading on the horizon like bad breath.

An hour later, flaccidly knee-deep in sines and tangents while listening to the rain maniacally tap-dance overhead, she just magically appeared.

"Hello?" Billie Jean asked, stepping into the kitchen. "I knocked but no one answered." My jaw fell open but absolutely nothing came out. "I'm meeting Sarah here to study."

Dripping, angling her head waiting for me to speak, her long lashes were dusted with glitter as tiny stickers, a peace sign and disco ball, groovily flanked her eyes. And with the wet fabric sucking to her braless torso, it was like she wore a lick from a bloodied tongue, rather than a redly ribbed tank top.

And then the cuckoo lapped up the seven o'clock hour. After the last ribald chime, she moved those retro amber eyes back to me and pointed at it.

"Do you know your clock sounds like it's giving a massive blowjob?"

Dizzy, since most of the blood in my body was currently going to power my new hard on, I pointed upwards and spoke. "She's upstairs."

"*Adios*, Daddio." After blowing me a wink that almost knocked me over, she was gone. And after spending ten aroused minutes processing what just happened, I closed my eyes to begin yet another erection eradication.

"Okay, Grandad, let's eat some more cottage cheese. Large curd though, this time."

Sea Trials

by BJ Condike

T he sea was calm despite the forecast of a fifteen-knot easterly breeze. The three- to five-foot swells predicted from the rising wind would be perfect for testing the new gyroscopic stabilizer I had installed on the *Anything Goes*. Pablo and I were conducting sea trials of the 48-foot trawler in the waters south of Stock Island. When the boat rolled from side to side in rough water it had made my wife seasick. I hoped the stabilizer would eliminate the motion and protect her from future suffering. It was either that or I had to sell the boat.

"What's taking so long, Frank?" Pablo called from the helm.

"Keep your serape on, Pablo. I'm still calibrating the inclinometer. What about your end?"

"Don't talk to me about serapes, *gringo*, or I'll take siesta twice a day." He grinned. "And the flywheel's not at ten thousand rpm yet."

Pablo worked full-time for me in my insurance business. He was still learning and made lots of mistakes, but he spoke fluent Spanish and interfaced easily with the local Hispanic population. He doubled as first mate on the *Anything Goes* when I needed a hand, like I did that day.

Pablo swiped through his phone to kill time. "Hey Frank—Crazy Eddie's on another one of his rants."

I grunted as I focused on reading an instrument dial.

"He's really pissed. Something about Karen stepping out on him."

"People shouldn't discuss their personal lives on Facebook."

"He's on Twitter."

"It doesn't matter!" What did matter was Eddie knew about his wife's extramarital activities.

"He says he's going to get even." He paused. "What do you suppose he means by that?"

"I have no idea," I said.

But people didn't call him Crazy Eddie for no reason. Eddie was a Haitian immigrant and used car salesman, one of those excitable characters who would leap on a car in a television commercial and bust out a windshield with a sledgehammer. "This is Crazy Eddie," he would yell, "and I'm smashing prices!"

"Well, he is your brother-in-law…"

Eddie's wife Karen was my wife Cindy's sister. They were beautiful, passionate, and as close as two coats of paint. Things were about to get messy.

We were heading south between Key West Airport and Boca Chica Key, toward the choppy waters of Hawks Channel. Pablo pointed west to the Hyatt residence club.

"Frank—look."

A single-engine prop-driven aircraft flew over the four-story building doing barrel-rolls. That wasn't normal.

"What the hell?" No sane pilot would perform a stunt over residential buildings like that.

I glassed it with our 10 x 50 binoculars. Navy surplus optics yielded a bright image that popped into focus.

"That's not a civilian aircraft," I said. "That's Eddie's P-51 Mustang." The image of the vintage WWII fighter plane grew larger as it approached. Eddie had painted the menacing face of a shark on the forward fuselage, its snarling jaws dripping blood.

Eddie had evolved from being an auto mechanic to a used car salesman, but along the way he acquired a private pilot license and became a certified aircraft mechanic. He had worked on restoring the WWII fighter plane for two years. I didn't know he had finished it.

The P-51 ceased its barrel-roll and began doing loop-de-loops—not the smartest move in a 70-year-old aircraft. I couldn't see how Eddie would 'get even' performing suicidal acrobatics in an antique airplane, but then again, he was crazy.

"That man is nuts," Pablo muttered.

"No shit," I said.

The fighter plane leveled out at a low altitude and headed in our direction.

"What's he up to now?" Pablo said.

The P-51 came at us broadside at no more than fifty feet above the water. The ancient aircraft engine roared overhead. The plane's propeller wash stirred up the water as it passed, creating a wake like a motorboat and spewing spray like a rain squall.

The new gyroscope did its thing and the boat barely moved despite the turbulence. Eddie wagged his wings in a classic pilot greeting which I interpreted more as a jeering taunt.

"Jesus! That man is certifiable!" Pablo had to yell above the din.

The war plane banked left and then veered right into a sweeping circle and headed back at the *Anything Goes*. Pairs of thin white geysers preceded its approach, the twin colonnades of water rising and fading in resonance with a staccato *rat-tat-tat-tat* emanating from the plane.

"What the fuck? Is he shooting at us?" Pablo shouted.

That's exactly what he was doing. Eddie's restoration must have included making the armaments functional, which had to be illegal. Who do you complain to about that? I might not live long enough to find out.

"Duck, Pablo!" I yelled as I dove and hid behind the gunwale.

We both sprawled on the teakwood deck as the fighter plane approached. The sounds of gunfire, breaking glass, and ricochets reached our ears. The engine noise faded into a Doppler whine.

I peered at the bow from my hiding place. Several smoking bullet holes punctured the foredeck and forward hatch.

"What the hell is he doing?" Pablo screamed.

"Getting even," I said.

"You mean you...and Karen? Your sister-in-law? What about Cindy? What were you thinking, man?"

"I wasn't, I guess." It just sort of happened. We bumped into one another at the gym. Maybe it was the sweaty bodies, or all that Spandex. We met for a latte after, and one thing led to another. And another. It was pheromonal. We couldn't stop.

Sea Trials

Eddie repeated his three-sixty turn and headed back toward us.

"Pablo! Life jackets!"

We donned our PFDs and tried to gauge where Eddie would aim next. We guessed the stern and rushed to the damaged bow.

The engine noise of the P-51 rose in pitch, playing harmony to the *chug-a-chug-a-chug-a* melody of twin .50-caliber machine guns. Bullets ricocheted off brass fittings, and teakwood splinters exploded everywhere. Odors of gun smoke and cordite filled the air as the blazing gun barrels streaked overhead.

"We gotta get out of here!" cried Pablo.

I jumped to the helm and slammed the twin diesels into full throttle and pulled a U-turn. We took evasive action and serpentined toward the Stock Island Yacht Club, figuring even nutso Eddie wouldn't attack us there.

But Eddie was faster. He strafed the bow a second time, perforating the engine compartment. Both diesel engines coughed, sputtered, and died.

Without propulsion we were stranded and exposed like sitting ducks in a Bedard painting.

"Launch the dinghy, Pablo!"

We dashed to the fantail and scrambled to launch the Zodiac inflatable. I shook so much I couldn't untie the knots tethering it to the trawler.

"Here he comes!" Pablo warned.

Eddie had come about and was headed at us again, this time from the rear. At that angle his machine guns would slice the trawler in half from stern to bowsprit. The dinghy didn't stand a chance.

I yelled, "Abandon ship!" and leapt over the starboard gunwale, while Pablo hauled his ass over the portside.

We bailed just before Eddie and his P-51 Mustang zeroed in on the *Anything Goes* and peppered it with .50-caliber cannon fire.

A 700-grain bullet traveling at 3,000 feet per second punches its target with 13,000 foot-pounds of force—enough, said the investigators, to rip apart an 800-pound flywheel rotating at 10,000 revolutions per minute in a near vacuum. A thousand screaming shrapnel fragments punctured every part of the trawler including the fuel tank. A pyrotechnic tracer round ignited the fuel, and the resulting explosion and fire did the rest. The boat sank in less than five minutes. The *Anything Goes* had gone and went.

The Coast Guard rescued us soon after. Pablo and I survived with a few scratches and minor burns.

Crazy Eddie headed southeast and flew fast and low below radar range. Maybe he made it to his native Haiti, or maybe he ran out of gas over the Straits of Florida. It's 735 air miles to Port au Prince and the P-51 had a flight range of 750 miles. Subtract out what he had burned in his aerial acrobatics and making to Haiti would have been a close call. He might have had to swim the last few miles. No one ever saw him or his P-51 Mustang again.

The *Anything Goes* hadn't been the only one on a sea trial that day. Crazy Eddie acted as my judge, jury, and executioner. He found me guilty and exacted what he saw as just punishment for my crimes.

Sea Trials

Not that he was wrong. I had been guilty—of cheating on Cindy, and of betraying my friend and brother-in-law Eddie.

Of course, Cindy left me, and cleaned me out in divorce court. And Karen won't speak to me—both for Eddie disappearing and for me hurting her sister.

I had to let Pablo go. He had failed to pay the premium on my boat insurance as instructed, so the *Anything Goes* became a total uninsured loss. Plus, the Coast Guard sued me to remove the vessel's sunken wreckage as it posed a hazard to navigation.

If I ever buy another boat, it'll be a small one. I'll call it *Everything's Gone.*

Son Cubano at ICE Amphitheater, Islamorada

by Rod Aldrich

The rhythms from two continents
pulse from the pavilion
over the throng.

At the back of the sparsely filled benches,
she stands facing the music,
a dory watercraft roped
to the docks.

Parts of her move:
fingers thrum,
hips tilt,
shoulders undulate.
Syncopating only
to the degree she suspects
her seated partner won't notice.

He's a driven down timber
bracing the stolid dock,
his back to the throbbing crowd
below the benches.

Son Cubano at ICE Amphitheater, Islamorada

What moors her?
Mental tethers?
She bucks against hers
in the undulating surf.

Maraca waves
curl upon the drumming barnacled rocks,
punctuated by strumming splashes
and cymbals hissing along the margin of
sand.

Suddenly she stills,
her shoulder length hair
the last to halt,
remnant bubbles
slide by the beached hull
back out to sea.

The House that Iggy (Re)built

by Lesa McComas

The house was a bargain by Key West standards, marketed euphemistically as a "project house." I'm sure the city would have preferred it be torn down and rebuilt on stilts above the flood plain instead of continuing to squat at sea level on its pre-climate-change, highly questionable slab, but that kind of project wasn't in the budget. I had to stretch to buy the "fully furnished" foreclosure, and was inexperienced enough not to initially grasp the full ramifications of its leaky roof, spalling concrete, and long-term termite damage.

"Welcome back, Cupcake," Del said, the day Kevin and I arrived to survey the situation, locksmith and electrician in tow. "Guess you know what you're in for here."

Del lived next door. Of indeterminate age, broad in every visible dimension, and missing a mismatched assortment of fingers, Del also sported a perpetually surly expression, an extensive collection of illegible tattoos that I hoped he hadn't spent a lot of money on, and a dirty black ball cap, from the back of which escaped a few tendrils of greasy mullet. I barely noticed any of it because he had been a friend when I needed one.

"Thanks, Del. Wish I could say I was glad to be back, but well, you know."

He nodded awkwardly, and I introduced him to Kevin. We made awkward small talk in the driveway for a few minutes while we watched the locksmith remove

The House that Iggy (Re)built

the front door lock and Del's hyperactive terrier attempted unsuccessfully to mate with Kevin's leg. It was quickly obvious that Kevin had taken an instant dislike to both our neighbor and his dog.

"Del isn't a bad guy," I told him later. "You should give him a chance." Del had moved into his house back when Key West was still a sleepy fishing town, and although he never had anything remotely complimentary to say about any of the island's residents, visitors, businesses, attractions, or government officials, still insisted he would never leave alive.

"He looks like a goddamned Hell's Angel. Not exactly Mister Rogers' neighborhood around here. And wasn't he buddies with Frankie? I just have a bad feeling about that dude."

Frankie Lee was the previous owner, and his shady history had undoubtedly helped to scare away potential buyers. Frankie had disappeared without a trace several years back. The newspapers called him a missing person, but as best I had been able to determine from my sources in city government, no one in the KWPD was looking very hard for him. Everyone knew that Frankie was into smuggling square groupers, and undoubtedly knew a lot of bad people.

Unconfirmed but persistent rumors of even more questionable goings on in the canal house probably contributed to the aggressively cheerless neighborhood. Half of the basic cement block houses in the block sported dirt yards guarded by large ill-humored dogs who threw themselves with gusto against their rusty chain link fences whenever I walked by, and the other half—the ones that had been converted to rich people's second homes—were sequestered behind bougainvillea-covered cement walls, biding their time until the rest of the neighborhood caught up.

Frankie had left behind a yard that resembled an abandoned petting zoo, and not in a good way. A shallow pond in the front had played a starring role in three increasingly contentious visits from county mosquito control inspectors. It featured several inches of mud, vegetation, and rainwater the color and consistency of week-old leftover guacamole. An arrangement of empty cages with tightly spaced mesh suggested former residents of the scaly or slimy variety, and the backyard was so closely packed with spiky, stabby, thorn-encrusted vegetation that we had so far only fought our way down one narrow path.

The inside had been little better than the outside. Kevin gave out a low groan when we first crossed the front threshold to survey my new acquisition.

"Did it look like this when you lived here?"

"Pretty much." Although it now smelled considerably worse thanks to several years with the electricity turned off, it looked almost exactly as it did the last time I saw it, right down to the empty pizza box on the coffee table, a few mummified crusts poking out. *Pepperoni and sausage.* Frankie always was a pig.

Using my phone as a flashlight, I went from room to room, surveying the same disheartening collection of mildew-stained brown plaid furniture, long-dead houseplants infested with defunct insect colonies, empty margarine tubs, rusted fishing lures, Jimmy Buffett cassette tapes, frayed sun hats, and vintage XXL Hawaiian shirts. After the electrician had verified it was safe to turn the power back on, we were pleased to discover that two of the house's four window air conditioners still worked, albeit in a grudgingly exhausted way, and Kevin agreed to take on the task of finding something to augment them before summer arrived.

The House that Iggy (Re)built

A few months earlier when Zillow alerted me that the house was finally on the market as a foreclosure sale, I knew I had to buy it. Because my income and a small inheritance let me qualify on my own, Kevin couldn't really argue, but it was clear he was hurt by what he saw as my abandonment of him and our perfectly good Miami apartment with its fully functioning appliances and plumbing. While we figured out what came next, we were keeping both the apartment and this mildew-infested wreck of a house three hours away from his job, our friends, and the nearest Whole Foods. But the complicated logistics of two households, coupled with the sheer scale of what was becoming an intimidating renovation, were already putting a strain on our relationship.

We had spent every spare moment our first few weeks in town filling a dumpster and salvaging what we could for a yard sale. We had gradually worked our way toward the back patio that featured a rusty but still functional washer and dryer and an assortment of mismatched outdoor furniture. At the end of each long day, we'd sit out there, try to imagine what the canal looked like behind that impenetrable wall of hostile vegetation, and toast our incremental progress with a couple of cans of Coors Light. We kept the beer cold in our "beer refrigerator," a bait cooler that had floated down from the boat ramp, refreshed every few days with a new bag of ice from the Dion's gas station and fried chicken emporium down the street.

I was clearing off the shelf over the washing machine when I found it. "Kev, look, a gun!"

Kevin walked over to look. "A pellet gun. I had one of those when I was a kid." He was the most excited I'd seen him since our arrival on the island, so I handed it over.

"Is it worth anything?"

"Are you kidding? I'm keeping this baby." Ignoring my dismayed look, he scanned the contents of the shelf and triumphantly retrieved a tin of gun oil and a can of pellets.

"I'm going to clean this off and see if it works," he said, heading out to the back yard.

A few minutes later I heard, *crank, crank, crank, crank...crank, crank...pffft!*

"Whoo hoo!" Kevin's shout sounded like it came from an excited 12-year-old. I heard the crack of dead vegetation as he hiked deeper into the yard.

*Crank, crank, crank, crank...*silence.

"Ugh!"

"What?" I asked, alarmed. "Are you OK?"

"I'm fine. Is there a shovel?"

"Uhhh..." I knew there wouldn't be one. Del had promised he'd get rid of it just in case anyone ever came looking.

I looked at the wall displaying rusted tools hanging on rustier nails. "We have a rake, if that helps."

"Can you bring it over?"

I cautiously picked my way through the yard, following his voice until I could see a horizontal sprawl of sea grape slumped over a decaying concrete seawall. Next year's project, maybe.

"Oh my god!" I gasped, covering my nose. "That smell!"

"The good news is, I found where it's coming from. See under here?"

I turned around, resolutely refusing to look, although I could hear the pack of excited flies buzzing nearby.

"Just tell me."

The House that Iggy (Re)built

"It's a huge iguana, maybe five feet long, nose to tail. Been dead a few days, looks like."

"I'll take your word for it." I handed him the rake. "What are you doing?"

"I'm going to toss him in the canal. Feed the crabs."

"Is that...OK? What if he washes up somewhere?"

"He'll sink. Consider it a burial at sea. Very earth-friendly, and the remains will be gone by morning. Do you want to say a few words in memoriam?"

"Pass."

Kevin unceremoniously tossed the iguana in the canal, and I joined him to peer over the side into the water. I could make out what looked like a shredded turquoise bandanna tied around what passed for its neck.

Kevin must have seen it too. "Was he...someone's pet? Why would anyone want a pet iguana?" he asked.

"It's kind of a Key West thing," I answered uneasily. *No way. Definitely not Iggy.*

The next morning, Kevin left early to check out a few leads on air conditioners. Carefully balancing my coffee cup, I retraced the path back to the sea wall to check on the crabs' progress with not-Iggy and take a few bracing breaths of jet exhaust before logging in to begin my workday. I was lucky that my remote software engineering gig let me work from anywhere.

"Sniff...Ugh." My coffee rose in my throat. *Not just jet exhaust this morning.*

The dead iguana was back, sprawled on the broken concrete a few feet from where he'd been the evening before. I put down my coffee and poked the carcass back into the canal with the rake Kevin had left propped against a nearby palm tree.

"Wow, weird," I said under my breath, peering into the water to make sure he went down and wasn't trying to climb out again. The water was murky from the incoming tide, and I couldn't make out whether the turquoise bandana was still visible.

Of course, it had to be a different iguana, maybe the grieving mate of the one from yesterday. He -- I decided I'd call him "he" because I never did know how to tell boy iguanas from girl iguanas -- lay belly up on the bottom, his legs and tail waving peacefully in the current. *Definitely not Iggy.*

Realizing I was about to be late for my morning online scrum, I quickly downed the last of my coffee and headed back to the house.

By the time Kevin burst through the back gate late that afternoon, I had finished my last meeting of the day and was up to the tops of my industrial rubber gloves in debris cleaned out from the garden shed. I knew the shed had been nearly empty the last time I saw it, and figured Del had been responsible for providing all these rusty cans and piles of trash. *Smart move. Nobody would want to touch this stuff if they could help it.*

"Am I the man, or am I the man?" Kevin crowed. "I scored two practically brand-new AC units from Habitat for Humanity. Let's go celebrate at Green Parrot. Popcorn is on me. We'll get them in the windows tomorrow before I have to head back."

"You are the best," I said, meaning it. It was only early March, but the temperature was already starting to climb. I dropped a few more rusted cans of scary looking chemicals in my growing pile and gave him a quick kiss, avoiding touching him with my rubber gloves.

"Help me pack this stuff up," I said, handing him a pair of gloves. "Tomorrow is hazardous waste drop-off day, and I knocked off early to get this stuff out of here." *The shed has to be emptied before we can do anything.*

Good God, look at all this crap," Kevin said, and I heard tape being unrolled to assemble a box. "Why did your uncle think flammable solvents and piles of trash were a good combo? We're lucky this shed hasn't spontaneously combusted."

After the initial sound of a few cans being dropped into the box, I didn't hear anything for a few minutes, and stuck my head out to find Kevin holding a newspaper.

"Hey, check out this article about Uncle Frankie."

"Please stop calling him that. Seriously, it's getting old," I said irritably, taking the paper. I was becoming convinced that Kevin just reminded me of the relationship to goad me. Although Frankie had been my mother's brother, it wasn't exactly something I wanted to advertise. Or think about.

"Key West Fisherman Donates to Sister Season Fund," read the headline.

"Frankie was a fisherman? I thought you said he was a drug smuggler."

"Frankie wouldn't recognize a tuna if it came in a Star-Kist can," I said absently. Fishing, with its fleet of boats coming and going, provided the ideal cover for his illicit maritime activities.

I scanned the article. The accompanying photograph showed two smiling men holding up a large replica of a check. The older, beefier of the two sported a large bushy moustache and was leering into the camera through aviator sunglasses. I was surprised by my fury at the sight of the man but kept my face a neutral mask.

Kevin knows the part of the story about my time living with "Uncle Frankie," the one that I've told all the people who are closest to me. A young woman, lured by the promise of cheap rent for a gap year in paradise to earn money for college, realizes she's gotten herself involved in drug smuggling and worse and cuts her stay short, a little older and wiser, but sadly not much richer.

Only Del knows the part where that young woman shows up on his back porch, half naked, bruised and sobbing, and cradling a dead iguana in her arms. That was the first night Del rescued me, gave me a pair of jeans that I rolled and cinched with a piece of rope, watched solemnly while I dropped Iggy into the canal, and then drove me to the police station, and finally to Marathon to catch the night's last bus back to the mainland. And only Del knows about my last visit, the one that came a few months later, after it finally became clear that the police were never going after Frankie for what he had done to me. To Iggy.

One more chapter to go, and I will finally be able to close that book and start a new one, where I turn the worst thing that ever happened to me into the beginning of my—our—new life.

"Frankie always knew how to stay in the good graces of the city's movers and shakers," I commented as I finished the article and tossed the paper in the recycling bin. "That's how he got away with so much."

Kevin returned to filling the box with cans while I dumped papers and beer bottles into the recycling bin.

"You know this shed is exactly where we might want to put a pool or a tiki hut someday," mused Kevin a few minutes later. I found myself cheered by his use of the word "we."

"Why don't I help you get rid of it?" he added. Half the yards in our end of town featured similar sheds, which were small enough to slip through the cracks of the city's onerous permitting process.

"I need it for, uh, storage," I said vaguely, wishing I had foreseen this conversation in time to come up with a better argument. Kevin was right, and the prefab shed on its gravel pad was clearly more of an eyesore than a feature. But, for the time being it needed to stay.

The House that Iggy (Re)built

"Well, OK, but how about I help you move it over there by the fence?" Kevin suggested. "I'm sure it comes apart."

"Sure," I countered, uneasily. "Maybe your next trip down here."

On Sunday night, Kevin was headed back to the mainland to work at his office for a week. That should give us plenty of time, I hoped.

I went out to the driveway to kiss Kevin goodbye and wave as I watched his taillights disappear into the twilight. A few minutes later, I heard Del's front door open, and he came out to stand quietly beside me.

"Got you a housewarming gift." I looked up to see he was holding a shovel. "Figured we could give it a test run tonight."

"Thanks, Del. I don't know how to..."

"Shhh, it's fine. Forecast says tomorrow calls for light winds and seas under a foot. Good day for a fishing trip out past the reef."

I took hold of his arm and we stood there for a few more minutes, watching the light fade as a flock of white ibis poked their sharp beaks into the dirt in search of dinner.

"See you out back at midnight," he said finally, before I heard him trace his steps back up the gravel to his front door.

Poinciana's Tears

by Linda L. Moore

It rained orange flower petals on my sky-blue Mini Cooper today as I sat inside crying.

This morning while sipping coffee in the cockpit of my sailboat, sunlit wavelets sparkling like diamonds caught my attention and I wasn't so sad. But it began to envelop me again, the sadness smothering me like a hug held too, too long. My sadness sucked away my happiness and erased thoughts of to-do lists that I kept trying to write so that in busyness I wouldn't feel anything, and I wouldn't totally flake out. I got out of bed and brushed my teeth and hair. I made coffee. I asked for a hug as I do every morning from my husband and with it three kisses, always three kisses. He's five inches taller than me and has muscular arms and I feel safe and loved when I can nestle into his hugs.

I met a friend at Croissants de France on Stock Island. I thought I was ready to be out socially without crying. It didn't go so well, but she knew what it was like to lose someone. Another hug. Looking for solace or answers or understanding, I drove my car to Elizabeth Street and turned into the free parking lot at the Key West Library. I was in search of a book on grief. Sure, I could buy the book by Elisabeth Kübler-Ross on Amazon or Thrift Books, but I didn't want to have it on my bookshelf—a permanent reminder of Jon's death. I would rather not think he's really gone.

Poinciana's Tears

The woman at the reception desk said, "That's a long walk." when I told her the online catalog indicated the book I wanted wasn't in the stacks but in Big Pine Key. Her chatty demeanor quieted when I told her the name of it, *On Death and Dying*. She arranged for the book to make its way to Key West. I wondered—does someone toss it on their car seat and drive it to this library?

I walked across the gravel parking lot, grateful for the warmth and humidity of early June in Key West and reminded myself it was time to carry a sweater. The too-cool library sapped what little energy I had left. I sat in the car and for a split-second thought of opening the window to warm up but didn't. The darkly tinted windows offered privacy and I knew no one would see my lips quivering and my eyes overflowing with tears. I stared through the windshield and said out loud through my tears to God or whoever listens, "it's not fair." Waiting. Waiting for a comforting word that didn't come. But the poinciana tree came.

I watched as countless flower petals floated and dropped without a sound covering the windshield and the hood of the blue cooper in bright red-orange dapples. I longed through my sadness to feel their softness, just as I longed to touch him—my 31-year-old nephew, my brother's only child, Jon. His cheek for only a few more moments that day, was soft and warm and the only part of his body without tubes before the heavy silence and before his body turned cold, so cold. I opened the door and chose three, soft warm perfect petals. I carefully folded them into a tissue and placed them in my purse.

****

Linda L. Moore

We were cuddled on the couch, your head nestled under my chin. Your tiny perfect fingers grasped one of my own. Your warm infant body rested upon mine. The two of us breathing softly—Aunt Linda and baby Jonathan. Moments such as this melted my heart and flowed through my body as if you were my very own.

I didn't know then, in those early years as you were growing, that I wouldn't be able to have children of my own. No sleepless nights or parental worries for me.

Your wry wit and goofy smile always made me laugh. You never minded my hugs as a child nor as an adult. You would cross the room and come right over to me for one. I felt your gentle warmth whenever I was around you, only needing a smile and "Hey, Aunt Linda!" to know I was loved, too. Oh, to hear that again, just one more time.

I was blessed to witness your life's milestones—graduation, engagement, marriage, celebrating the birth of your daughter. And still, for me to have held you as a baby and known you as a man will always be our rare unbroken bond.

Poinciana's teardrops blanketed the Mini Cooper today as I sat tucked inside crying.

In Loving Memory of Jonathan Michael Moore
1990 – 2022

Anthems to Angels
On the Women of Tennessee Williams, or "Tom" in Key West

by Mia Shawn

Beautiful "Follies of God", your words.
Without Each, your void.
Your Anthems to Angels, never heard.

Without Her, lost.
No solace. No song. No words.
Silence, your cost.

Still, "from the Mist" She came.
Magical Muse. Inspiration. Heavens to hold.
Always, the same.

And once Her embrace, your Choruses to God!
Her gifts your Gilded Verse.
Eternity to trod.

A Key West Memoir

by Arida Wright

Everyone knows Key West is famous for writers: Hemingway, Robert Frost, Tennessee Williams, and Elizabeth Bishop, to name a few. I learned about the supportive writing community here while visiting as a tourist. I had a dream to become a published author. I arrived November 1, 1997, manuscript in hand. My shero Princess Diana died, and I realized we were the same age, thirty-seven. If I didn't pursue my dream then, I could die with all my writing inside.

I was like Dorothy, following the Yellow Brick Road; only when I got here, I had to find work, maneuver housing issues (moved ten times in twenty-four years), survived destructive romantic relationships, suffered through a miscarriage, had two divorces, was homeless twice, visited the psyche ward five times. Baker acted twice. I totally lost sight of the dream. These obstacles were my lions, tigers, and bears, oh my! Flying monkeys, falling asleep in the poppy field, the guard not letting me in when I finally reached Emerald City and the whole time, the Wicked Witch wanting to steal all the magic I had inside.

Four years ago, I was blessed to receive a scholarship to attend the Key West Literary Seminar. There I met a writer in my short story class who strongly encouraged me to come to the Key West Poetry Guild.

A Key West Memoir

There I met Flower Conroy who was the current Poet Laureate of Key West, and she invited me to attend her free poetry class at the library. My first day there I saw poets sitting around the table with their published books in front of them. I was determined this would be my destiny as well.

I was born in her class that day. It was an out-of-body experience as the brilliance came oozing out of me. I cried a lot that week because through Flower, I met my Glinda, the good witch who told me I had it in me the whole time to go "home." This was home. Poetry was home. And all the poems we wrote that week were published in an anthology by a grant Flower received from the Anne McKee Grant Fund.

The book signing at the library was transformational! I reveled in being front and center at the podium and receiving money in my hand for the book. Everyone loved what I wrote and how I performed. It was a high of all highs!

I began performing poetry at my church after the anthology came out. My church members were the first ones to buy the books Flower gave me to sell. It's difficult to put into words the feeling when someone puts money in your hand for words you wrote. Each time I performed poetry at church, I was invited to another church event, but the poetry I was writing and performing now were not the ones in Flower's anthology. They were radical poems, influenced by the piercing of my soul. Current events of how black people were being treated affected me very deeply and I took pen to paper to try and soothe the pain of having to watch the things on TV I was watching, read the things in the paper I was reading, engage in the conversations I was engaged in, and all the while a silent suffering kept me writing.

Each poem I wrote I took to the Key West Writer's Guild which I had joined finally after years and years of avoiding because I didn't want to be the only person of color in the room. I had already suffered this trauma when I was in high school. My mom took me out of an all-black high school, because I was getting in trouble getting high, cutting class, and hanging with the wrong crowd and put me in a white high school in a school district where she taught so she could watch me better. I totally hated her for this because I was one of 20 black students in my high school.

There was one white boy that got bussed in with the black kids. His name was Robert John McCormick. We became boyfriend and girlfriend, Bonnie and Clyde walking the hallways of hatred in 1975. No one ever hurt us, but the vibe was horrendous to walk through. So was the vibe when we walked together in my neighborhood which was black. His family never let me visit him inside their home. I always had to sit outside and wait for him to come out.

Today, in all the circles I move in in Key West, I am the only person of color, except for church. However, as hard as it is to read radical poems to the white members of the Key West Poetry Guild and the Key West Writers Guild, my radical poetry was praised, and I kept hearing the Guild president Rusty saying loudly, "Arida, you have a voice, a voice that needs to be heard past this room, past this island, to the whole world." With that in mind, my collection of poems will become my book I have entitled, *Crossing the Threshold: Voice of a Black Woman.*

A Key West Memoir

With each poem I am attempting to transmute the violence, the hatred, the malice I feel inside when our society shows injustice toward the black race. I am also attempting to strike a chord that vibrates with the reader and with people who hear my poems, that will allow them to cross over the threshold of racism in their own psyches which is what I had to do every time I went to the Key West Writer's Guild or the Key West Poetry Guild. I also have poems in the book that highlight the achievements of our race.

I am very grateful to Flower and to all the writers and poets who have helped me believe I can fly over rainbows. I appreciate the diversity I bring to the group. I would have cheated myself if I had continued to let the color of my skin keep me from going among them due to all the feelings of inadequacy I experienced and have overcome. Now, after all these years I see the wisdom of my mother, and I smile. I also smile as I remember the first few times I attended the Key West Writer's Guild; I went running out of there before the sessions ended like the Cowardly Lion and had full blown panic attacks in my car. I had to call my life coach and have her talk me down from the ceiling.

It's ironic to me that after all these years, the poems I took to them for critique are being published with a grant from the Anne McKee Fund. The fact that I was given the Richard Heyman award for the poems I submitted teaches me that there are blessings in brokenness and rewards when you gain courage from your colleagues to walk through your fears and face the Big Oz who was just a small man behind the curtain.

Arida Wright

The book comes out this winter and like the poets I saw in poetry class with their own books, I will have manifested the desire I had then. On that day, like Dorothy, I will click my heels three times and over the rainbow I will go.

Did You Go to the Beach?

by Laura Knight

"Tor- TU-U-U-U-ga Terry on Z-15, the Florida Keys' first and best rock 'n roll station. Folks, keep your eyes peeled for those lost dogs! Friendly German shepherd mixes, they answer to Sheba and Amie. Reward offered! If you see them call the Z-15 hotline at 294-0013." Terry started his next record, the instrumental playing beneath his voice. "And now, for the second week in a row, the nation's number one song on this steamy Saturday, 'Hot Stuff,' by Donna Summer."

He took the headphones off just as the phone rang.

"Z-15!" he zinged.

"Will ya stop talking about those dogs?" a man whined. "You haven't stopped yapping about them since last night!"

"Those are my dogs, and if you find them, I'll stop talking about them!"

Terry slammed the receiver down. He looked at the photo taped to the control board. Sheba, the reddish shepherd mix rescued from the streets of Miami. And Amie, purchased at the Sunrise flea market. The vendor said the fuzzy pup was a purebred German shepherd. Two months later, when Amie's ears refused to stand up, the lie was revealed. But she was so lovable. And Sheba took over the pup's education. No human effort went into her training.

Where were they? Laura must be pacing the floor, waiting for a call.

Yesterday started out as a fun Friday. When his shift ended at 1:00 o'clock, Terry headed for the shabby rented Conch house on Southard Street. After playtime with the dogs, he walked with Sheba to Sloppy Joe's. He tucked the canine under their customary table at the open-air door, his favorite spot for watching humanity passing by. Terry was sure that if he stayed long enough at that table in that island city, he'd see everyone he ever met. Once a high school classmate had walked past without noticing him.

Dogs weren't allowed, but Sheba, all 75 pounds of her, stayed discreetly under the table, bites of cheeseburger keeping her placid and quiet. After a couple of Miller Lites he took Sheba home and went to the dentist.

Two hours later, giddy on generous doses of laughing gas, Terry motored home in the capacious, dirty yellow, 1968 Buick 225. The 11-year-old car was too big for Key West, but it was paid for. Even high he expertly parked the car on the one-way street. Then he glided up the sidewalk, hoping Laura had already changed out of her work clothes. Her savings and loan required all employees, male and female, to wear tan and brown polyester uniforms, garb unsuitable for their favorite Friday afternoon hangout. The Top overlooked Key West from the uppermost floor of the pink La Concha Hotel. Best of all, now that it was summertime, the locals had it to themselves.

He opened the front door.

"The dogs are gone!" Laura yelled.

Did You Go to the Beach?

"Gone? What do you mean, gone?"

"They're not here! They must've crawled on their bellies underneath the house!"

Like most Conch houses, theirs was set on 18" concrete block piers, high enough so air could circulate underneath, low enough to keep the dogs inside the fenced yard. Or so they'd thought.

Terry checked the backyard for himself. The gate was latched. The dogs were indeed gone.

That sobered him up. "I can't believe this! They've never tried to go under the house before."

"Maybe they were chasing a cat." Laura fisted her hands in frustration. "Amie doesn't have a clue about traffic. She'll run right in front of a car. And Sheba might try to herd her. They'll both get hit!"

"I know, I know. At least they'll stay together."

"Good point. I can't imagine Sheba would let Amie out of her sight."

"Let's call the radio station. They'll announce it on Pet Patrol right away. Then I'll look for them."

"OK. I'll find a photo to take with you." Laura shuffled through an album. "Here's a good one!" She peeled back the plastic page protector and extricated a photo of Sheba and Amie lying side by side. "Why don't you show it around the neighborhood first?"

A half hour later Terry came back, shoulders slumped.

"No one saw them?"

"Nope."

Terry's stomach tightened as he imagined all the harm that could come to the dogs. Hit by a car. Poisoned. Worst of all, dognapers were snatching pets, taking them to Miami and selling them for their fur. Sheba's coat was especially attractive. Preoccupied with these thoughts, he hadn't noticed that Laura was almost crying; she must be envisioning the same catastrophes. He hugged her.

"We'll find 'em," he said, with far more confidence than he felt. "Do you mind staying here in case someone calls? I'll take the car and look for them."

"Make sure you go to the beach. They love the beach."

"But they've never been to the beach here."

"Remember how much they loved swimming in the canal when we lived on Big Pine Key?"

"Yeah. Sometimes Sheba dived in headfirst, eyes open. It was amazing." He tilted his head toward the radio. "Listen—that's Dead Air Dave, making our announcement. I'd better get going."

He drove west on Southard to Duval, where he turned right, all the time scanning both sides of the street. He parked the car at Mallory Square. Patchouli and marijuana scents overlaid the salty air. Slim young people clad in jeans and headbands were drifting in for sunset celebration. The crowd would be small, no more than fifty, all locals. The town had shrunk since the Navy pulled out, and this time of year there were no tourists. Iguana Man still showed up every day with two or three green, orange, and brown lizards. Iguanas were considered exotic; they hadn't become the invasive pests that would plague future Key West residents.

Terry worked his way toward the pier, showing the photo to all. He recognized many of the sunset watchers. Key West was the kind of place where even if you didn't personally know someone, you'd seen them out and about.

Did You Go to the Beach?

And a lot of folks knew him from the radio station. Everyone was sympathetic but unhelpful. He heard a speedboat and watched a water skier approach the ramp installed between Key West and Tank Island. Spectators whooped as the skier landed smoothly. Turning away from the water, he glimpsed a brown dog with Amie's familiar shape. But it wasn't his dog.

From Mallory Square he drove slowly past the shrimp docks, then through Old Town. He crept by the Casa Marina. The luxury hotel, closed for a decade, was undergoing a lavish restoration. He circled the cemetery. As the sky pinkened in anticipation of sunset, he ducked into a gas station to call the radio station.

"Hey man, got a lead for you," Dead Air Dave said. "A guy called; said he saw your dogs by the Poinciana Lounge."

"Thanks!" Terry rushed out and headed to Duck Avenue. He drove around the block that housed the Poinciana. There was little traffic, so several times he stopped the car in the middle of the street, yelling, "Sheba! Amie!" He turned the Buick and drove around the block again, from the other direction. No response.

He trudged into the tavern. An old Eddy Arnold tune played on the jukebox. Terry showed the photo to the bartender and the men occupying the barstools. They all shook their heads. He called the station again.

"Got another call. Someone saw them by the butcher shop."

Terry turned his headlights on and drove a few blocks farther, but once again no sign of the dogs. The butcher shop was closed. It was dark. Time to go home.

"I went everywhere I could think of," he explained to Laura. "I stopped to call the radio station; someone saw them by the Poinciana Lounge, but by the time I got there, they were gone. Then someone else saw them near the butcher shop."

"The one you do the ad for? 'You can't beat their meat?'"

"That's it." He shook his head. "Couldn't find 'em."

"Did you go to the beach?"

"I went to Mallory Square."

"Not Mallory Square, the beach! Did you go there?"

"No, by the time I was done in New Town it was dark."

Laura glared at him. "I would've gone to the beach."

They slept that night, but not much. Nightmares of vicious dognapers interrupted their slumber. Terry was already awake when his alarm sounded at 5:00 a.m. On the way to work in the early morning darkness he made a detour to Duval. Couldn't hurt, since Sheba knew her way to Sloppy Joe's. The bars had closed; their patrons had stumbled home or followed the taillights of fellow revelers to Last Flight Out, the airport venue open 24 hours a day. The streets were empty of traffic and pedestrians. Some blocks were downright spooky, most of their buildings unpainted and boarded up, retail stores that hadn't survived the Navy downsizing. Then there was the surprising effervescence of Fast Buck Freddie's, a newer, eclectic emporium in the old Kress building.

On every block, sleek cats strutted down the sidewalks or calmly washed their paws on the stoops. But he saw no dogs. Was there time to cruise A1A? He checked his watch. *Should've thought of that before.* Even in Key West it was radio sin to sign the station on late.

A few hours later, and his shift was about to end. He cued an oldie, "Mama Told Me Not to Come," by Three Dog Knight. The phone rang. Terry lowered the headphones to his shoulders.

"I think I found your dogs," a teenage girl chirped. "They're in my back yard, eating my cat food!"

"I'll be right there!"

Tad, the afternoon air personality, sauntered into the studio, Coke in hand. He wore sunglasses and was fragrant with the scent of marijuana.

Terry tossed the headphones on the counter. "I'm outta here!"

"But, but...I'm not on for ten minutes." Tad stood, mouth agape, holding the soda can in the air.

"Too bad! They found my dogs!"

He dashed out and sped to a single-story concrete block house off Flagler. Sheba and Amie were still devouring the cat food. They bounded to Terry as soon as they heard his resonant voice, leaping on their back legs and lapping his face with their tongues.

"C'mon guys, let's go home!" Terry laughed. The dogs raced to the car. Once secured, Terry offered the teenager a reward. She demurred, but he insisted. "I'm sure they ate $10 worth of cat food."

Back on Southard Street, another round of leaping and lapping when the dogs saw Laura. With a huge smile, she sat on the floor to keep them from pushing her over.

"Whew, you guys smell like fish! Were you down at the shrimp docks?" Sheba and Amie wagged their tails. "I wish you two could talk and tell us about your adventures! And you're not setting a single paw in the backyard until Terry gets back from Strunk Hardware."

"I'm going to Strunk Hardware?"

"You're going to buy lattice panels so these escape artists don't sneak under the house again!"

The next morning Laura savored her first sip of coffee as she opened the *Key West Citizen*. With a start she set her mug down and thrust her head closer to the newspaper, studying the above-the-fold photo in the Sunday feature section.

"Terry! Come here!"

"What?"

The photo showed kids and dogs playing on the beach. She placed her index finger on the image of a pointy-eared canine who stood ankle-deep in the water, looking directly at the camera.

"That's Sheba!"

Terry bent down. He touched the image of a dog who stood at the water's edge.

"And that's Amie's butt!"

Laura shook the paper. Hard.

"I *told* you to go to the beach!"

Party Night on the Bight

by Jennifer Juniper

Breeze fingers
pluck palm trees
making them sway side to side
bending to those first notes
the whispered whoosh
signaling a symphony
about to begin

Like the Charlie Brown girl
dancing by
bouncing her head
two counts to the right
then two counts to the left
the fronds her stringy black hair

The water was
a smooth glass dance floor
but not anymore
it shivers
shimmies
then quakes

Jennifer Juniper

Wind whips
summoning up waves
they begin to move
one direction
in a synchronized line dance
set to twangy country music

Then rocking out
chaotic as a mosh pit
until they find rhythm

Their pointing peaks
hands holding together
in a cotillion dance
joining, then separating
joining
then separating
cotton ball clouds are
big white wigs atop
corsets and hoop skirts

Lightning flashes within
the fluffy puffy white blue
from white wigs to the white coat
of a mad scientist
the scoundrel
clamping charging cables onto
his monster's bolts
zzt zzzt zzzzt

Party Night on the Bight

Lightning lines
blur and blast
into flashes of Mother Nature's camera
she's taking pictures of us
her children
for we will never be this age again

Flashes become more rapid
a celestial paparazzi
trying to catch me running out
to buy milk
without my make-up on

Joke's on them
nobody's going to buy those snaps
nobody cares
Fierce and brighter now
morphing into a strobe light
it's a midnight disco

A boom of bass drum
thunder cracks
making dancers of boats
who were wallflowers
hoping to hide
in their slips
a mast bell dings
calling a partner
It takes two to tango

Jennifer Juniper

The thunder rolls
groans
its restlessness
rumbles
in hunger

Raindrops kiss the channel
softly at first
flirting
then...

Stronger
searching
deeper
passionate now
desperate to join
making her surface bounce up
before
plunging down
into the juicy
innermost depths
of her bay bottom

The skyline's twinkling lights
chaperone
until all sight is blurred
in the deluge

Laila's Journey

by Josie Mintz

Sarah winced at the squeak of her bedroom door as she pushed it open, then shook her head. She had been meaning to oil those hinges for a good week, but twice now she had ventured to the shed to fetch the oil only to find herself standing in the middle of the dusty space with no memory of why she had gone there in the first place. Of course, it really didn't matter, she thought to herself, now that Lester was... Her throat constricted at the thought.

Crossing the room in a few short strides, Sarah tugged at the lower sash of the filthy window. It didn't budge. She heard the door squeak again but pretended not to notice the dog as she continued to pull fruitlessly on the warped and faded wood. If only she could get some fresh air, she could clear her head and her thoughts wouldn't be so muddled. A crow landed on the dormant branch of the old pecan tree just outside the window, startling Sarah and causing her to stumble backwards over the gangly pup.

"Now look what you've done!" Sarah exploded at the frightened animal.

Out of the corner of her eye, she caught sight of herself in the bureau mirror and the scene took her breath away. On one side she saw herself, wild hair hanging in disheveled strands that had come loose from her usually neat bun, eyes blazing with anger like a tiger ready to pounce. On the other side, nearly out of the mirror's frame, was the pup, trembling, cowering, her doleful eyes downcast as if mere avoidance of sight would allow her to become invisible. Sarah felt her rib cage constrict as deep, bellowing sobs escaped from her chest.

"Oh girl, I'm so sorry girl," Sarah cried, dropping to her knees.

She fumbled in her pocket and found a half-eaten granola bar. When she'd put it there, or why, she had no idea. But now she held it out to the terrified animal as an offering, desperate to prove she meant no harm. How could she have spoken to the dog, Lester's dog, so harshly?

The animal sniffed warily, fearing some sort of trick. Then, ever so slowly, she began to crawl on her belly toward Sarah's outstretched hand. Gently she took the proffered treat and Sarah began to stroke her soft fur.

"There, girl. See? Everything's okay. It's not your fault. It was that blasted crow that spooked me," Sarah crooned.

Thoughts of the crow caused Sarah's heart to race once again. Crows were a bad omen, everyone knew that. She glanced to the window to see if it was still there, but between the dirt-caked pane and the waning light, she could only make out a series of menacing shapes in the growing darkness. Panic rising in her chest, Sarah strained to hear the familiar *click-whoosh* of the ventilator, that inanimate machine that kept Lester here with her, suspended between life and death. She held her breath as the clock ticked off painful seconds that seemed more like hours. Sarah began to count, one...two...three...then, *click-whoosh*. Sarah let out a mighty exhale and crumpled on the floor, her tears drenching the soft, mottled fur as she cradled the pup and drifted into a fitful sleep.

Laila's Journey

Sara opened her eyes slowly, and for a moment, she wondered whether she was awake or asleep, so thick was the darkness that enveloped the room. Still disoriented, Sara felt the silky fur between her fingers and the hard, unyielding surface under her hip. Where was she? As her eyes adjusted to the darkness, Sara strained to identify the familiar shapes. The dog's soft muzzle pressed into her hand, snuffled her warm breath, but Sara pushed her away.

"Not now, girl."

Sara willed herself to cut through the fog in her brain. Why was she on the floor? Had she fallen? Hit her head? Is that why she had that strange ringing in her ears? She had to be more careful. If something happened to her, who would take care of Lester? She wished the ringing would stop. She forced herself to block out the sound and slowly the picture took shape. The window. The dog. The crow. Lester. She must have cried herself to sleep on the floor. Yes, that made sense. She was just exhausted. But then another thought. What had woken her from such a deep slumber?

And what was that dreadful ringing? With a start Sara realized that the sound wasn't inside her head at all. It was coming from the ventilator. She sprang to Lester's bedside, ignoring the dog's startled yelp. No! Oh God, no! The machine had stopped working sometime during the night. Sara quickly turned on the light and frantically smashed the button to start it again, slamming her fist down on it in frustration.

Sara began chest compressions, placing one hand over the other on Lester's lifeless chest, just as the home health nurse taught her. She steadily counted off thirty compressions. The rhythm of her counting steadied her some, gave her something to focus on. Gingerly she tipped back Lester's head, parted his pale lips, and checked his airway. She took a deep breath and went to a place deep inside herself, forcing herself not to think of Lester's tender kisses as she placed her mouth on his. She returned to chest compressions as torturous sobs choked her. Over and over she brutalized Lester's chest, willing him to live, damning him for leaving her. In the end, it was all for nothing.

Sara sat on the side of the bed, rocking back and forth as waves of grief crashed over her. Eventually the storm within began to calm and Sara wiped her eyes. She stood, needing to do something to distract herself from the devastating reality that threatened to settle in.

The next thing. Just do the next thing. And then the next thing after that. Her mother's words to her in childhood now became a mantra. "Next thing, next thing, next thing," Sara whispered into the darkness as she willed her leaden legs to take her to the kitchen. She took the phone from its cradle on the wall, felt its heft in her hand, leaned her hot cheek against its smooth, cool plastic. So many of her friends had gotten rid of their landlines, connected to the fancy cellular phones their kids bought them. Smart phones, they called them. Sara had no kids, and she had no use for a phone that claimed to be smarter than her. She never quite trusted a phone that wasn't connected to a cord. A cord was real. Solid. Something you could see and touch. You knew a phone with a cord would be there when you needed it. A cellular phone, on the other hand—who was to say? Her friends were always complaining about low batteries, or dead spots or some such nonsense. No, Sara would take a real telephone, thank you very much.

She pressed the numbers 9-1-1 and waited. Next thing, next thing, she thought to herself. She felt the dog's warm muzzle in her hand and absentmindedly patted her head. A voice came over the line and asked, "What's your emergency?"

Emergency thought Sara bitterly. What emergency? Lester was dead. There was no bringing him back.

The woman repeated her question, startling Sara.

"It's...Lester...he's dead."

"Did you say someone's dead, ma'am?"

"Yes. Lester."

"You're saying someone named Lester is deceased?"

"Yes."

"Are you sure the individual is dead, ma'am?"

Was this woman serious? Sara thought. Either a body was dead, or they weren't.

"He's dead," Sara snapped, louder than she meant to. "Can you send an ambulance or...or a...look, can you just send someone to pick him up?"

The woman agreed and Sara gave her address. The woman said they would send someone right away, but Sara knew that was a lie. She and Lester lived deep in the woods off of an old logging trail. That was the way they liked it. They wouldn't even have the telephone if it was up to Lester, but Sara had insisted. "What if one of us has an accident?"

The operator disconnected and Sara stared at the phone in her hand, dial tone buzzing like an impotent bee. The stupid phone that was there for emergencies, which was supposed to save them. Rage overtook Sara and she slammed the phone in its cradle so hard it bounced out and slammed against the wall, dangling from the cord. Her anger still unsatisfied, Sara looked around her. With one swipe of her arm she cleared the kitchen table of everything on it, papers flying, dirty dishes and silverware clattering to the floor.

Josie Mintz

Sara shook all over. What had gotten into her? This anger, this rage, it scared her. She fell to her knees as fresh sobs wracked her small form. Next thing, next thing, she thought as she slowly began to clean up the mess. As she scooped up a stack of mail, mostly overdue bills, a colorful brochure caught her eye. She picked it up and gently smoothed the creases. "Visit Key West, the Nation's Southernmost City" urged the sunny yellow letters overtop a background of palm trees and sandy beaches.

Lester had always dreamed of traveling to Key West. He would wax poetic about everything from conchs to Hemingway to islands full of bones to anyone who would listen. But Sara, ever the practical one, always had a reason they should wait. Money was tight, it was hurricane season, mosquitoes carried diseases, and besides, she didn't even know how to swim. Lester would listen patiently and eventually acquiesce with a sad smile and a little shake of his head and the words, "Maybe next year." Then he would kiss Sara on the top of her head and amble out back to his workshop.

Sara looked again at the shiny brochure in her hands. She had sent away for it, written an old-fashioned letter on paper with an envelope and a stamp. She didn't really expect the department of tourism to reply. But she had been saving her money, shaving little bits here and there off the grocery bill, because she had planned to surprise Lester with a trip. Sara had been excited when the tourism people sent her a bunch of brochures. She thought this was the prettiest one of the bunch. She had planned to make Lester a special birthday breakfast and sneak the brochure under his plate. But then he got sick. And he didn't get better. And then there were doctors and tests and bills piling up and the *click-whoosh* of the ventilator and any thoughts of a trip were pushed aside.

Laila's Journey

Suddenly Sara was struck with how tired she was. She didn't have the energy for this. Struggling to her feet, she headed back to the bedroom, still clutching the brochure.

"C'mon girl," she said as the dog obediently fell into step beside her.

Sara trudged back to the bedroom. There was nothing to do now but wait. She climbed up on the bed and curled up next to Lester and she didn't even object when the pup jumped up beside her. Sara closed her eyes and pictured Lester smiling, beckoning to her from sparkling turquoise water. She fell asleep dreaming of Lester and Key West.

The month after Lester's passing was a blur. The first few days, Sara had barely had the strength to get out of bed. She didn't bathe or change her clothes. She barely ate. Her only exercise came in the form of short trips from the couch to the door to let the dog in or out. By the end of the week, she had miraculously managed to throw together a small memorial service for Lester. A few neighbors showed up to offer condolences, but Sara honestly couldn't recall their names. Later, some ladies from the Baptist church where she held the memorial (the only one she could get on short notice) stopped by, requisite casseroles in hand, only to be disappointed with Sara's unenthusiastic response to both their culinary offerings and their concern for the state of Sara's immortal soul.

By week two, Sara slowly began to make small steps back toward the land of the living. Strangely, it was Lester who coaxed her back, despite the fact that he had plunged her into the darkness to begin with by dying on her. Each night he visited her in her dreams, beckoning to her, encouraging her to get up, to keep going, to do...something. She just wasn't sure what. It was the pup that finally solved that riddle for her. It was the day Lester's remains were delivered. They arrived with the mail. Two bills, a limited time offer from a credit card company, and the ashes of her soulmate.

So this was it, she thought. This was what a life amounted to—a few pounds of dust and some assorted mail. Sara tossed the envelopes on the counter and gingerly placed the parcel that was Lester on the table. Taking the scissors from the drawer, she carefully cut open the packaging to reveal the small, basic urn she had chosen. It was simple. Practical. It was Lester. Or was it? Pictures from the past sprang unbidden to Sara's mind like an upended keepsake box spilled upon the floor. Lester in his workshop putting the finishing coat of stain on a plain, but exquisitely crafted pine table. Lester's smiling face as he pulled the blindfold from Sara's eyes after a surreal, sightless trip up the mountain to surprise her with the tiny cabin they would soon call home. The first time she laid eyes on her love—how handsome he looked in his Park Service uniform, the picture of safety and stability. Sara was vaguely aware of the pup's swishing tail brushing against her leg as more scenes came into view, ones she had not given much thought to at the time but which now, somehow, seemed to possess great import. Lester reciting the vows he had written for her, describing the beautiful, free-spirited artist he had fallen in love with. Lester coaxing her from the pile of dirty dishes by pulling her into his arms and dancing with her to a song on the radio. The normally reserved Lester looking like an excited little boy after the first day of kindergarten when Sara relented and said they could go look—just look, mind you—at the litter of free puppies advertised on the general store bulletin board. And finally, Lester, frail and soft of voice, looking up at her from their bed, cupping her face in his hand, apologizing for the life he imposed upon her, the life he thought extinguished the bohemian flame that had burned in her soul.

"Oh, Lester, what am I supposed to do now?" Sara sobbed, caressing the urn.

****

"C'mon girl, we're here," Sara beckoned to the pup trembling in the front seat of the battered old Chevy truck.

"It's okay, you can jump down. See? It's not that far."

Sara felt in her pockets for some sort of bribe, but she came up empty. She was losing patience with the animal, but she tried not to show it. After all, it wasn't the dog's fault, she reminded herself. Both of their worlds had been turned upside down since Lester got sick. At least Sara had some level of control over her situation. Lester's poor puppy, on the other hand, she had no choice but to go along with whatever decisions Sara made for her. And Sara's decision had been to find her a new home.

It had seemed like the right thing to do at the time. Now Sara looked down at the trembling black dog crouched in the torn and faded seat of the old truck. The animal looked from Sara to the ground, then back to Sara again and Sara's heart gave a little squeeze. No, she had to do this. She couldn't reconsider. It was best for everyone. But as the pup's sad brown eyes held Sara's gaze, she couldn't shake the feeling that everything about this was wrong.

Steeling her resolve, Sara reached into the truck, grabbed the dog's collar, and gently tugged. The pup reluctantly jumped down from the cab and walked with Sara, pressing close to Sara's side. They trudged up the drive to the front of the house and Sara rang the bell. When no one answered, she rang again, then finally knocked on the door with her fist. Eventually she heard a muffled voice yelling from inside the ramshackle house. The door swung wide, and Sara's senses were immediately and violently assaulted with the smell of urine and stale cigarette smoke.

"Yeah?" asked a small, stout woman as she took a drag from a fresh cigarette, lest the odors emanating from her house lose their pungency.

"Bonnie? I'm Sara," she offered her hand.

Bonnie's only response was a blank stare and another long drag on the cigarette. Sara stifled a cough and tried again.

"We spoke on the phone? About the dog?"

The pup began to whine and hid herself behind Sara's legs.

"Your ad on the bulletin board said you did boarding and fostering," Sara said, losing patience. "I called you over a week ago and you said you'd take her."

Another whimper came from the pup. Sara's anxiety was beginning to skyrocket. She needed to get this over with so she could get back home.

"And I told you to bring her right over," Bonnie replied, thrusting her cigarette at Sara for emphasis. "Now I got my hands full with some pregnant bitch my neighbor dumped on me that's about to whelp."

Sara hesitated. When she saw the notice on the board, this had seemed like the perfect solution. The pup got a good home and Sara was relieved of the responsibility and with a clean conscience to boot. Now that she had met Bonnie in person, her conscience was feeling increasingly grimy.

"Fine, I'll take her but I ain't got all day," said Bonnie finally, with an exasperated sigh. "She's got plenty of breeding years left in her. She ain't fixed, right?" She asked as she grabbed at the dog who cowered behind Sara and gave a soft growl. Bonnie jerked her hand back. "She bite?"

"Of course not. Just give her a minute to—" Sara began.

"No more minutes. Shit or get off the pot." Bonnie interrupted with a scowl.

Sara looked down into the big brown eyes of the frightened pup and realized exactly what she had to do.

"Come on, girl," Sara said, turning around.

"Wait," called Bonnie sharply. "Ain't you leaving her?"

"Not on your life," Sara called over her shoulder without looking back.

Sara's heart was pounding as she made her way back to the rusted red pickup truck with the pup bounding happily at her heels. Not confrontational by nature, Sara had encountered bullies all her life and had never once stood up to one. Not until now. There was no way she could leave Lester's dog with that horrible creature.

****

Sara's newfound confidence lasted until she was about halfway home. Then the tears started. What was wrong with her? Would she ever stop crying? She had always heard that grief came in waves, but hers was more like a raging sea that utterly engulfed her. She wondered if one day it would drown her completely. Sometimes she thought that might not be so bad. She was so tired, just...so, so tired. She looked at Lester's urn still sitting on the table. She hadn't found a good spot for it yet. Just one more decision she couldn't seem to make. She poured herself a glass of water and sat down across from Lester.

"This is all your fault, you know," she snapped. "You were the one who wanted to live in the middle of nowhere off the grid. You were the one who wanted a damn dog."

Somewhere inside Sara sensed a dam breaking, but she couldn't stop.

"And then what do you do? You fucking die on me, that's what. How dare you?"

She slammed her hands on the table so hard the urn threatened to topple, but she didn't care.

"What am I supposed to do now? What am I supposed to do about the bills and the house and a mangy mutt that needs to be fed and a truck that's falling apart? Tell me, Lester! Tell me what I'm supposed to do!" she screamed as she threw her glass at the wall in frustration.

Sara slumped down in her chair and beseeched the silent urn as hot tears burned her cheeks.

"Please Lester, please. Just tell me what to do. I can't do this alone."

She felt an insistent nudging at her knee. Irritated at the pup's intrusion, she thrust out a hand to push her away.

"I'll feed you in a minute," she said, sharply.

But the nudging came again, this time with a scratch of paper across Sara's skin. Startled, she looked down to see what the pup had gotten hold of this time. She reached for the paper just as the pup dropped it into her lap. It was the brochure for Key West. Sara stared at the wrinkled, glossy paper in her lap, then looked back at the pup, who was cocking her head in such a way that it could almost be understood as a question.

"You want to go to Key West? Is that it, girl?"

Laila's Journey

Sara laughed at the absurdity of the idea. Sure, maybe at one time she had dreamt of traveling to exotic places, but those days were long gone. Then again, Key West wasn't exactly a far-off exotic land. Hell, it wasn't even another country. Maybe? Oh, who was she kidding? She had only left the state twice in the last decade. Once for a funeral and another time for a wedding. Lester drove both times. Sara let out a weary sigh.

"I suppose you want dinner."

She headed to the kitchen, shaking her head and chuckling to herself at the idea of her traveling to Key West alone. But now firmly planted, the idea refused to be uprooted, instead weaving its tendrils in and through the deepest corners of her brain.

One month later Sara found herself behind the wheel of Lester's rusty, red Chevy pickup truck with a duffle bag and backpack containing her remaining worldly possessions in the back. The pup rode shotgun. Lester in the cupholder. As she navigated the battered vehicle down the old logging road for the last time, Sara glanced down at the wrinkled Key West brochure on the dashboard and took a deep breath. A burst of movement from above caught her attention as a crow landed in a tree up ahead.

"We got this, right?" she said, looking at her travel companions.

The pup barked and Sara smiled. She stuck her arm out the window and flipped the crow off for good measure as she drove by.

"How about some tunes?" she asked as she flipped on the radio. An Eric Clapton song came on. "I guess if I'm gonna keep you, I gotta give you a name."

She looked at the pup, thoughtfully.

"Laila. I like it. It suits you."

Josie Mintz

She affectionately scratched the pup behind the ears and was rewarded with a sloppy kiss. Sara's heart felt warm and light. That was the funny thing about journeys, she thought. When one ends, another starts. Lester's journey would end in Key West. But for her and Laila, the next thing was just getting started.

Big Key West Decision

by Dick Moody

We got our start in the art supply business in Florida in 1983, We purchased a one thousand square foot art and engineering supply store, essentially drafting supplies in a small strip center in Altamonte Springs on the outskirts of Orlando. This was for one simple reason, it was in the Yellow Pages with an existing phone number and address, and had retail fixtures. It was not for the existing business.

We added many fixtures, acquired the empty store next door, and ordered $50,000 worth of art supplies, framing equipment, and artist furniture. I acquired the rights to an art catalog from a friend in Washington, DC, and modified it to suit our new inventory and store.

Add a cash register, and ArtSystems of Florida was in business.

We hired a counterperson away from my competitor. My wife Kathleen was an accountant, and I was the purchasing agent, in charge of advertising. Business took off, mainly because my two competitors knew very little about commercial art supplies and we had the right inventory, the catalog and now an outside salesman. "Free delivery—call before 10 am, receive before 4 pm" kept the phones ringing off the hook

I hired another floor salesperson with a fine arts degree, and we had exactly the crew we needed. My son, Wyatt, graduated from high school and between deliveries he turned out to be one hell of a salesman. We had a huge sale one Saturday a month with sodas, keg beer, and "ArtDogs," and along with our direct mailer we packed the store.

I often worked seven a.m. to seven p.m , six days a week, Kathleen and Wyatt nearly as long. We tried to take weekend breaks.

Kathleen and I sailed our 37' Hunter sailboat from the gulf coast of Mississippi where we had a home and I was the art director of the Naval Oceanographic Office. One of the advantages of that location was its proximity to New Orleans. We took the one-hour drive to the French Quarter as often as we could.

Good friends of ours, Brad and Linda Kamp, with whom I often played music, mentioned how much fun their visits to Key West were and how similar the art and architecture were to New Orleans. We researched the Fantasy Fest events and we were hooked. We worked out the dates and arranged to take off the Halloween week in October. We made reservations for a room in a guesthouse on Duval Street.

We packed up my 1965 Porsche 911 and arrived Monday about two p.m. I pulled up in a parking place in front, opened the hood to retrieve our two suitcases and a shoulder bag with costume materials. I was about to enter the gate when the owner, Dennis Beaver, who is still a friend of ours, bound over the sidewalk waving his arms. "You can't park there, there are no other Porsches in Key West and people will steal parts off your car."(remember this was 1986). He continued, "You can park in my spot in the back and your car will be safe."

Kathleen looked at me. "Dick, did we make a mistake?

"No honey, we will park in the back and I have the car cover."

Big Key West Decision

We had one of the best weeks ever, and we had traveled many places in the world. Every morning I crept downstairs to Croissant de France for coffee and French pastries. We visited galleries, museums, live music and jewelers. We met writers, realtors, painters, sculptors, street musicians, jugglers and local costumers who were happy to share their Key West tales with us. After the big Saturday night parade and a nightcap we left the party and returned to our room.

We left before dawn and took Route 1 to the turnpike and from there, 100 mph to Orlando. Kathleen slept. When she woke up, I said to her, "Hey honey, would you like to move to Key West?"

"I thought you'd never ask!" She leaned over and kissed me. It was a done deal.

***

We returned to Orlando, sold the business, and moved to Key West in 1988. We bought a gallery on a quarter acre at 910 Duval Street and several years and several properties later, we are still here...

There is No End.

Early Morning Michelangelo
A Morning in Key West

by Mia Shawn

Anonymous youth,
the Early Morning Michelangelo.
To the biased, uncouth.
Yet with Dignity's Music you roll.

White picket specs,
hardworking man.
Sliding strokes of paint like last night's sex.
Diligence, all you can.

Fences you may find
won't hold the summits you
will climb.
Soar!
Early Morning Michelangelo.

Let Us Pray

by Joanna Brady

On balmy breezy mornings, you can usually find me walking along the White Street Pier to greet the day. When I go early, it sometimes means stepping carefully around the sleeping bodies of people who come down to Key West in winter to escape the raw cold of mean streets and subways in northern cities. Our homeless snow birds.

For me, the pier has special meaning because of the AIDS Memorial at the entrance.

My brother Tony was gay. Not "raised pinkie" gay; not even "limp-wristed" gay. He was flaming, and proud of it. He'd had the courage to come out in the 1950s when he was just twenty-one, at a time when there was no such thing as gays—just family men with hidden secrets. A choice he rejected.

A writer of published short stories and a world traveler, Tony was an activist in Toronto in the '70s and '80s. He had a vivid imagination and was always coming up with ideas to improve his community. He was also persuasive, the kind of person who could get people on board to help him carry out some of his fascinating schemes. A born leader.

One of his more memorable ideas was the Forsythia Festival in Toronto. One year, he went door to door in his neighborhood and asked everyone to plant a forsythia, the first shrub to show color in the spring. Soon his corner of Toronto came to life with glorious golden flourish, proclaiming an end to the long dreary winter. He got the City Council to match each shrub by planting one in the nearby park. In appreciation, the Council honored Tony with a plaque in the park, and a public lane they named after him. The Festival lives on to this day and has become the focal point of an annual neighborhood fair.

Tony was several years older than I was. Growing up, we were a close family, and my brother and I shared a particular bond, more like a sisterhood than your usual brother/sister relationship. He was a very funny guy. You never knew what kind of crazy thing or silly joke he'd come up with. I was his "straight" (in more ways than one) who laughed at most of his witticisms and gags. When I had my own family, he became very much a part of it, and my kids loved him.

So, when Tony died of AIDS, we were all devastated. He had always loved Key West, so when I moved down here, I arranged to have his name etched on a stone at the AIDS Memorial on the Pier. Nine stones in, fourth from the top. Every time I pass it, I silently say hello, and even confide things to him. (Yeah, I'm a little eccentric, too.)

This one day, I saw two of the awakened "lodgers" of the Pier in an argument over the Memorial. They were grubby and scruffy, and the punky, ripe odor they gave off was hard to take at that hour of the morning. Just standing near them made me itch all over.

"I tell ya—it's a war memorial," declared one of the pair, the taller, older guy with greasy shoulder-length hair and a huge cross dangling from his neck.

"Nah, Rev, I don't think so. I think it's fer somethin' else," said his bud.

I should have let it pass, I suppose. But I'm a born eavesdropper. And a busybody. I had to enlighten them.

Let Us Pray

"It's an AIDS memorial," I informed them.

"AIDS, hey? Well, now whaddya think of that, Shorty?"

"AIDS? They put up memorials for that?"

I was afraid they'd start in with disparaging homophobic remarks, so I hurriedly added, "My brother's name is on it."

That turned out to be a mistake. They insisted I show them where Tony's name was inscribed, and I did.

"We're gonna say a prayer for 'im," said the guy with the cross.

It was an offer I couldn't very well refuse. The next thing I knew, the "reverend" had asked me my name, and before I could stop him, he took my hand. Shorty took my other hand, and we formed a little circle over Tony's inscription. One Human Family, I thought, echoing the official motto of Key West. I glanced around to make sure no one I knew was cycling by as we bowed our heads.

"Dear Lord in heaven," the reverend intoned, "accept our prayer for the fine gentleman remembered here, and for his little sister, left on this earthly soil to mourn 'im..."

I thought he was done, but no, he droned on for another five minutes or so, invoking various denizens of heaven, including A-list prophets like Isaiah and celebrity angels like Gabriel and Michael. He threw in a few saints for good measure. The length of his oration made me think that perhaps he had really once been a clergyman.

I thanked the pair for participating in this bizarre early morning ritual. It was kind of magical in its own way, and I actually felt uplifted. I wondered how Tony would have reacted. With his quirky sense of humor, I had to think he'd have roared with laughter at this odd tableau—his sister and two homeless dudes praying over a slab of stone with his name on it, absent any of his remains.

There was a squeal of gulls as a flock of them landed near the monument. The sun was up, and a southeast breeze was rising. Over the wind and sounds from the sea, I thought I heard a low familiar chuckle as I left.

Did I mention Tony was an atheist?

Only in the Keys

by ML Condike

My phone rang the 1930s tune "We're in The Money." I'd reset it from Beethoven's 5th Symphony three days ago when Carl booked our first event in the Keys. A guy named Joe Burns, a retired banker we'd met once at Coco's Kitchen, placed a last-minute order. Apparently, the Key Deer Boulevard venue for his daughter's wedding reception burned Sunday night.

March first, a month ago, we'd packed and left Cleveland on a whim. After sleeping in our utility trailer crammed full of catering supplies a few nights, we rented a houseboat at the Old Wooden Bridge on Big Pine Key while we looked for affordable housing. Catering was our backup plan if we couldn't find suitable part-time work.

Nothing materialized for us. Rent was gobbling up our savings fast and we were damn sick of fish. So we came out of retirement, resurrected our business, and named it Lucky Rooster Caterers.

Last Friday we'd tacked tear-off business cards on local bulletin boards all over Big Pine Key, including Winn-Dixie. And Tuesday we got Joe's call. He'd grabbed our card there. Being seasoned businessmen, we celebrated our good fortune hooking a banker.

"Got it Frank. It's probably Joe Burns. He was scrambling to find a new venue. Gave me his credit card. Said he'd call back with the venue address once it was finalized."

I nodded and kept working on the final prep.

Carl waved a scrap of paper. "Sends his apologies. Slipped his mind amidst the chaos."

"Talk about last minute. Start loading. I'll finish here. Can't stop or we'll be late."

Sniffing the Swedish meatballs, I tossed a pinch of allspice into the sauce. Last-minute prep always took longer than expected. I dusted the eclairs with powdered sugar, then packed them single-layered to keep them neat.

Once loaded, we headed north on Overseas Highway. After two and a half miles, I veered right onto Long Beach Drive, a mangrove-lined road leading toward the Atlantic. Yellow signs warned of Key Deer crossing.

I slowed the van to a crawl. "Are you sure this is right? There isn't much out here."

Carl read his note. "It's one...something ...something...seven."

"What do you mean something, something?"

"Can't read my writing. I'll check the order slip." Carl grabbed the reservation book from the console. "Joe mentioned an inn or B&B."

I glared at Carl.

"Sorry, Frank."

I glanced at the dash clock. "Cripes. It's late."

"Relax. We don't serve for a half hour. Much farther and we'll be in the ocean."

"You're right." I nudged the gas pedal. Edging along, we searched for a driveway or a sign. My hands shook. If we aced this reception, maybe we'd get a big tip and more clients. A banker like Joe Burns probably knew everyone.

"There it is!" Carl gestured toward a vine-covered sign. "The hmm...Inn...I can't read the name. House number's one, five, five, seven."

Only in the Keys

"The first and last digits match. Check and see if you wrote fives."

Carl stared at his note. "Could be. Sorry Frank."

"Let's chance it." I entered the gate and coasted down a crushed coral drive.

"Door's open." Carl unbuckled his seatbelt. "This must be it. I'll grab the hot food."

I backed up to the building. "I'll check inside."

Sweat dripped from my chin as I rushed toward the door.

"Whoa!" I stopped short almost colliding with a naked man exiting the building.

"May I help you?" His skinny legs supported a turnip-shaped body. A hairy chest topped his flaccid belly that drooped over his privates like a loincloth.

After I cranked in my eyes, I blurted, "We're here to serve dinner. Sorry we're running late. Where do we set up?" I bit my lip to squelch a grin.

"Follow me." His body quivered with each step. Inside we found rent-a-tables and chairs arranged in clusters. He led us into a well-lit kitchen.

Carl's eyes twinkled as he placed the hot-food carrier on the counter.

The naked man stretched right and then left like an athlete warming up. "Is it a buffet?"

"Of course. That's what you ordered."

"Perfect." We turned when the back door opened. A woman joined us from the raucous beach party. "Hey, Val. Glad you made it."

The attractive, naked "Val" waltzed over. Every sensuous muscle of her firm slender body flashed in the kitchen lights. She opened the food carrier door. "What do we have here?"

"Dinner," I croaked, nearly swallowing my tongue.

"Great. I'm starved." She swirled around and left, rejoining the beach party.

Carl and I watched Val vanished into a wavy sea of skin and hair.

The kitchen smelled of institutional cleaners. Still, after seeing unclothed bodies roaming outside, I sprayed the counters with odorless disinfectant before rolling out butcher paper.

"Start bringing in food while I set up the buffet."

"Got it." Carl hustled out.

Uneasy, I turned to the naked man. "Is it okay to remain dressed?"

"Absolutely. Visitors wear whatever they want. Holler when you're ready."

"Great." I wasn't keen on serving in the nude.

"Ta-ta for now." He joined the noisy throng outside.

After twenty frantic minutes setting up, Carl closed the hall door and fanned his face. "It's sweltering in here. No A/C. I'm stripping to my underwear. I certainly won't stand out in this crowd."

He shed his pants and shirt, then slipped into extra-light, serving whites.

I contemplated doing the same, but I'd worn my new Good Luck Undies, the ones with the red roosters all over them.

One night at Hogsbreath in Key West, a rooster landed on our table while Carl was in the restroom. He roared when he returned. Since then, he'd teased me about my "meet-up" with a chicken. Yesterday, he gave me the boxers.

The scarlet and brown fowl would show through the thin serving whites. So, I resisted stripping down. But the temperature kept climbing.

"This is unbearable!" I mopped my face with a paper towel.

Carl danced a jig. "I'm comfortable."

"I give! I can't stand it." I stripped to my rooster boxers, then slipped on my whites.

"Ah...Frank. A rooster's pecking your ass." Carl laughed.

Grinning, we donned our chef hats and proceeded to the hall.

Carl stuck his head out the door and shouted, "Food's ready!"

A steady stream of naked men and woman filed in. Everyone carried a towel over his or her shoulder and placed it on their chair before sitting.

"I wonder which one's the bride?" I whispered. Nobody seemed pink-cheeked and giddy, although, a lot of cheeks displayed themselves. And nobody was hanging off the arm of a handsome, young thing wearing nothing but a bow tie.

Carl scanned the crowd, then shrugged. "Good question."

The serving line continued for what seemed an eternity. Almost fifty people. Good thing we made extra. All sizes, shapes, and colors of bare bodies moved past as I scooped out meatballs, rosemary potatoes, and French-style green beans. I fought to keep myself from staring.

Thirty minutes into serving, and three refills of the warmers, my phone rang "We're in the Money."

"Who's calling now?" I hesitated, but the number looked familiar. So, I pressed "accept."

Before I could speak, a gruff voice said, "Where the hell are you guys? You said you'd be here an hour ago."

"What?" My heart plummeted past my rooster shorts and landed south of my knees. "Who is this?"

"It's Joe Burns for Pete's sake—the whole damn wedding party's in the reception hall waiting to eat. Where are you?"

Wide-eyed, I looked at Carl as I spoke. "We're at One-Five-Five-Seven Long Beach."

"You idiot. I'm at One-Six-Five-Seven Long Beach—the Key Deer B&B. A quarter mile further." By now he was shouting.

I covered my phone. "Shit. We're supposed to be at the Key Deer B&B."

"You're not serious." Carl frantically scraped the remaining meatballs into the corner of the chafing dish and looked at me. "Not much left."

"What a screw up." I uncovered the phone. "Mr. Burns...I don't know what to say."

"Say you're coming for Christ's sake! My wife's furious. My daughter's sobbing in the powder room. The groom's smoking pot on the beach. And the in-laws are packing up to leave."

"I'm not...um...there's been a major mix up." My new Good Luck Undies didn't feel so lucky now. In fact, I was fighting to keep the roosters clean and dry.

"What kind of mix-up?" Burns sounded about to cry.

"We served the meal to another group." I paused. "I'll send something over."

"You better! And make it fast!" He hung up.

Burns had estimate 35 attendees including the wedding party. Damn, I should've been suspicious when we served close to fifty nudists.

"What now? Pizza?" Carl asked.

"Quick thinking," I said, then estimated four slices per person. "We'll need at least eighteen large pizzas. You get ten and I'll get ten. Better be safe than run out of food. You call Island Pizza on the Overseas Highway."

Only in the Keys

"On it." Carl started punching his phone keys.

Pizzaworks at Winn-Dixie Plaza promised five pizzas in 45 minutes, so I said go ahead. Then I called the No Name Pub and told them the story.

After the guy stopped laughing, he said, "They got you too."

"What do you mean?" My neck hairs lifted.

"We bail out caterers regularly. The Bare Barn Inn nudies love a free meal."

I was speechless.

Carl tapped my arm. Held up five fingers, then a quick three, then five.

I gave him a thumbs up and added his remaining five to my order.

"I need ten large pizzas, half cheese and half meat lovers, delivered in forty-five minutes. Deliver them to..."

"I know where they're going." He chuckled. "I'll donate some garlic bread sticks, too."

"Fantastic." I gave him my credit card number.

I looked at Carl's hang-dog face. "We'll never live this down."

"Sorry, Frank."

We stood sober-faced next to last ten meatballs when the naked man strolled over. "I'm sensing some bad vibes. Is everything okay?"

"No. It's not."

He cleared his throat. "By chance, were you headed to the Key Deer B&B?"

"Yes!" Anger crept through me.

He smiled and shrugged.

"But you already knew that." My neck burned.

"We love getting a free meal from time to time."

I fought to keep from punching the guy.

He grinned and thrust his hand in the air. "Club members, club members. Quiet, please."

The crowd settled down.

"Give thanks for this donation—such an exquisite meal. And offer well wishes to the bride and groom at Key Deer B&B."

An applause rolled through the crowd like a wave at a ballgame.

Shocked, I barked, "Just a damn minute. There's no way Joe Burns is going to pay for this. You knew this food wasn't for your nudie beach party. Plus, I had to order twenty pizzas on short notice. You need to pay."

He calmly raised both arms toward the heavens. "Did you hear that, folks? Joe Burns' daughter got married."

The crowd responded, "Halleluiah."

Val rose and glared at the naked man. "Bare Cubs, we need to talk."

Carl muttered, "What in hell? I've heard of the Sanibel Naturists, but Bare Cubs?"

As if rehearsed, the entire club stood. Each member grabbed their towel and left the hall.

Val pointed her finger at me. "You wait here! We'll be right back."

Where'd she think I'd go? I still had wedding cake and 70 éclairs in the kitchen probably melting by now.

Within ten minutes the crowd returned, each nudist waving currency.

Val collected the cash as they re-entered the building.

When the line ended, she handed me the stack of bills. "It's obvious you old guys are a low-budget operation and new to the Keys. We're not bottom feeders. We only fleece deep-pocket revelers who rent Deer Key B&B for private orgies. Here's a thousand dollars. It should cover your costs, including the pizza, and give you a small profit."

Someone shouted, "Use it to buy white underwear. Your roosters are showing."

As the laughter subside, eight male Bare Cubs, terry sarongs draped around their bodies, emerged from the kitchen. One carried the wedding cake. The rest had trays of éclairs.

Their leader shouted, "Come on Cubs. We have a delivery to make."

The rest of the members stood, wrapped themselves with their towels and formed a line of half-naked bodies. The entourage left singing their version of "The House of the Rising Sun."

"There is a house on Big Pine Key.
It's called the Bare Barn Inn.
It'll be the ruin of two old cooks,
And God I bet it's them."

I grabbed several spatulas, and a cake server. Carl clutched bags of paper goods. Then we raced out the door to follow the parade.

Cars filled the lot at the Key Deer B&B.

Carl pointed to a sullen middle-aged couple loading suitcases into their Mercedes. "That must be the in-laws."

The nudist parade and two pizza delivery trucks flooded into the lot. The No Name Pub delivery car whipped in and clogged the driveway.

"You can't park there," the father-in-law yelled. "We're leaving."

"We won't be long," a delivery guy shouted.

The in-laws commiserated. Curiosity must have got them. They fell in behind the dessert crew walking into the hall.

We scurried ahead to find Joe Burns. He was easy to spot. Paunchy. Red faced. Wearing a tuxedo. Before I could speak, the cake-carrying nudist approached.

"Sorry Joe. Foods on us." He handed me the cake and said, "Be right back."

I looked at Carl and he shrugged.

A hush fell over the room as the parade of half-naked people filed in and circled the perimeter.

Their leader stepped forward. "Ladies, gentlemen, bride and groom. It's with great pleasure that we join this celebration." He nodded to the Cubs.

As if choreographed, the girdle of half-naked people raised their arms one-by-one, letting their towels drop to the floor.

Gasps escaped from the guests.

Before Joe Burns could react, the nudists shouted in unison, "Pizza for everyone!"

When the leader's arms lowered, each nudist grabbed a towel, and threw it on their shoulder.

The stunned wedding party watched with mouths agape as the naked cavalcade left.

Carl and I served pizza and listened to the hall buzz for the rest of the evening.

After the reception, Joe Burns joined us carrying an envelope. "I wasn't going to tip you. But wow! What a show!"

"Thanks," I said, as if we had anything to do with it.

"My daughter said she'll never forget her wedding."

I looked at the roosters peeking through my serving whites, then at Carl.

"Only in the Keys."

Love Nest

by Patty Tiffany

spring comes early in Key West
orchids erupt starlike lushness
frangipani show off perfumed petals

as the sun gawks across the sky
burns our feet on hot white sand
waves go flat, breezes lay down

the season of loud laughing gulls,
perched on the concrete pylon
outside our floating home

each morning of April
they squawk, nuzzle beaks,
stare at me, at each other

a loving rendezvous
without a plan
migratory mantra maybe

but no TV, no internet
just standing together
on spindly black legs

uncomplicated, shared preening,
slipping their mate silvery sea creatures,
paired for life's season

Patty Tiffany

slipping away at dusk
to an avian palm island boudoir
a feathered paradise

nothing to stop
their mating mission
the sultry shared springtime
gulls Intent on their purpose

The Great Mediator

by Dale Dapkins

I first met my next-door neighbor across a hurricane fence separating our two properties. He was sunning by his pool stroking the mutt in his lap. I didn't want to disturb him, but he looked up when his little dog growled.

He said, "Oh hi. I'm Dave, Detroit Dave. Youse must be Dale."

Cradling the mutt in his left hand, and extending a hairy right hand, he shook my entire body. He stood five foot-six and weighed close to 300 pounds. Patting his belly, he chuckled, "Mom says I gotta lose weight."

Second generation Cuban American via Detroit, Dave wore Cuban shirts unbuttoned all the way down to his pubis, where polyester shorts displaying a menagerie of parrots, flowers, and fish, took over. Bare feet.

"Mom likes to buy my clothes—from catalogues."

Most days Dave sat by his pool, his black chest hair outing itself like an invasive species looking to root someplace it wasn't supposed to. A thick gold chain hung from his neck supporting a three-inch ebony cross upon which an ivory Jesus was nailed. Whenever he found things beyond comprehension, he'd clutch the crucifix in his right hand, and his little dog, Stinky, in his left. Gazing skyward, he'd beseech the Almighty. "Why? Just tell me why, Lord."

He bore a strong resemblance to Manuel Noriega, the acne-scarred Panamanian strongman who Reagan

Dale Dapkins

blasted with heavy metal after locking him up when he wouldn't give us back our canal, the one America built in the first place.

Me and Dave bought our places in the nineties. Dave with a suitcase full of cash. Me, a cashier's check. You get a bigger chunk of land here in New Town, and easy parking. I got four cars, five if you count my Harley Knucklehead. Dave had only a silver Mercedes. His Mom liked my Harley parked in front of their house. "Makes burglars think someone's home when Dave's away "on business."

A year later, we were old friends who met and complained regularly across our fence about life. I was telling him how I'd lost big bucks going for extra cash to buy this Baywatch fishing boat with four tuned Toyota 225 outboards—a little birthday gift I was giving myself. I'd gone all-in buying AOL on a Monday. By Wednesday AOL was in Warren Buffet's short-sell toilet.

"Youse bought AOL after Mom told ya not to?"

Looking skyward, clutching his cross, he beseeched Jesus. "Why do I even try?"

I whined, "Jimmy The Greek says, if you're losing, you double your bets. Always worked before."

"*Stupido pinga*! Da Greek was talking about blackjack."

"Anyway, I need some source of income—a job. "

"If youse want, I'll make some phone calls. Maybe my old job is still open."

"Thanks, Dave, I appreciate it, but that's alright," I said, remembering the week before when Dave and I were passing a bottle of Havana Club back and forth over the fence. He'd confided, "Don't tell nobody, but the last 20 years I worked special ops for a health insurance company."

"Special Ops?"

The Great Mediator

"How do I put this? Sometimes an insurer needs to call in an independent contractor—you know, a specialist—to "unsubscribe" a hypochondriacal type subscriber who's draining their books with high medical bills. Well, you're looking at that specialist."

"Jesus, Dave."

"It's a living. But you can't do that shit forever, man. Ya come home, and your dog's licking brains off yer socks. You got bad dreams. Mom sees I'm unhappy, so she enrolls me in one of these on-line lawyerin' schools. I take the course. Now I'm legit, right? Working with the law instead of fighting it. Hey, it's a beautiful thing. A month later Mom says people are telling her that I should look into the mediation racket—for a side hustle. So she signs me up for that too. And now, guess what? I got lawyering money and mediation-money coming out my ying-yang."

"You're kidding!" I said, relieved he'd moved on from getting me his old job with the insurance people and, of course, I was intrigued by money coming out my ying-yang.

"Yeah, ya just go up to Miami and take the class."

"That's it?"

"Yup. That's it, then announce that youse is a certified mediator and ya start rakin' in the dough. Maybe ya print up some fancy business cards. 'Mr. DALEY BOY Esquire – MEDIATOR. Forty years' experience. Lowest price in Florida.'"

Anyone in Key West can hang out a shingle offering oddball shit: palm reading, astrological maps. Down the street, Astrid, the lady with one arm, claims an alligator ate it up in Boca or sumpin'. She peddles Island Life guidance, whatever that is. Free mangos when ya sign up.

"Ya just take the week-long mediation course they give up in Miami."

Dale Dapkins

"A whole week? Jeeesus, Dave."

"Hey. Like Mom says, Rome wasn't built in a daze."

Dave gave me the key to his "Professional" office condo in Miami Beach Gardens where he had two months left on his lease.

My Transformative Mediation class met every morning in an empty storefront in Liberty City. A 70-year-old lady with spiked gray hair wearing a loose-fitting man's seersucker suit taught it. The pants had urine stains.

To protect identities I'm giving my classmates fictitious names; there was Mouse-Girl, skinny with a razor thin Bonnie Raitt mouth, wild curly hair. She started out shy but grew less so as the seven days passed.

Bigfoot was her opposite, a heavy, hairy, raw-boned gal from Wisconsin. Though she laughed like a donkey, I could tell she was the kind of gal you could phone late at night to go your bail.

Next was Buzooms, an older lady with a massive chest riding atop spindly legs, which did not look like they could support such oversized bags of Christmas jelly, which jiggled when she laughed. I imagined a passel of grandchildren (and me?) pressed against her pillows as she read Runaway Bunny with heartfelt tenderness.

Then there was Queequeg, your typical Pakistani or Sri Lankan or whatever he was. Like Ismael's harpooner, Queequeg's face, hands, and body (I assume) were covered with tattoos.

Me, Queequeg, and Will Rogers were the only men. Will Rogers was a tall, lanky cowpoke who favored rockabilly-style shirts embroidered with horses. He wore a black Stetson, which he kept parked on his desk like a pick-up truck. Snaps instead of buttons closed his shirt, which he tucked inside crisply ironed blue jeans. Though stooped, he was maybe six-foot-six in his cream-and-green ostrich boots. Will seasoned his speech with soft y'all's as if addressing an old friend who'd turned up unexpectedly at his door. "Y'all come on in now."

Mrs. Tupper introduced herself, "I'm Mrs. Tupper—just like your mothers' Tupperware parties," she said, laughing as if anyone other than Bazooms knew what that was. She wore rhinestone cat's-eye glasses, and a quivering fake smile.

"People, this is YOUR mediation course. My job is to teach you transformative mediation. And I WILL do that. But while I'm at it, I will try to keep you from being swallowed by the rising seas of arrogance. Anytime you want me to help you out of your quagmire of ignorance, please don't be afraid to ask."

Bigfoot raised her hand.

"Not now, sweetheart," snapped Mrs. Tupper.

Bigfoot's hand sank down.

"As you familiarize yourselves with the tools of transformative mediation—" Her phone rang. She paused, flashed a fake smile and after listening, said to the phone, "Okay, just do what you have to do."

She hung up and continued. "You will be amazed at your new powers." She glanced at Queequeg. "That said, I warn any of you hoping to become some sort of mystic psychological guru who hands out dishonest resolutions for money: NOT ON MY WATCH!"

Then she said to Queequeg, "You, sir. That phone call was about you. There's still time to leave and get your money back."

Queequeg got up and quietly left the room.

"Wise choice sir! Okay, where were we? So, with transformative mediation, we pride ourselves in guiding our clients toward wholesome resolutions that they, themselves create. Even if a solution seems obvious to us mediators, we resist imposing it upon them. I make it clear that if at any time I am not addressing their issues, to say something."

Bigfoot's hand shot up.

"Not now, please!"

The hand went down.

"A word of caution: if you let clients start bickering like children, it'll never stop. Believe me."

Her phone rang. She checked the caller and let it go to voicemail.

"Where were we? Okay, upon first meeting with my clients, I ask each of them to clearly state their position on the issue they want resolved. Then, as moderator, I'll re-state what I believe each one said. For example, 'So, client one, what I hear you saying is, 'blah blah blah.' Do I understand that correctly?'"

She went on to explain the whole mediation process. We did a lot of role-playing exercises. Mrs. Tupper would act as mediator between two students assigned the role of clients. After five minutes, Mrs. Tupper would choose a student to replace her as mediator, and two different students to play the clients. Mrs. Tupper would then retire to the back of the room to cuddle with her phone.

Each night, we went out to dinner as a group. Mrs. Tupper never joined. At our first dinner together at Chez Louis Restaurant, I saw that I might have judged some personalities wrong when Will said to the waitress, "Gimme a double Jack Daniels straight up, Doll."

After taking all our orders, the waitress went around the table checking that she had the orders correct. When she came back to Will, he said, "That's right, Sweetheart, mine's a double Jack."

When Mouse Girl stared at Will, he asked, "What's wrong, Dahllin?"

The Great Mediator

Buzooms answered before Mouse Girl could respond, "I think she has a problem with the way you addressed the waitress."

"Well, suckyouuuuuuuuze me!" he said feigning indignation.

"It's disrespectful, that's all," said Mouse Girl quietly.

"Way I see it, most gals I know don't mind getting compliments," said Will.

"Speaking just for myself, I wouldn't mind if some hunk called me Honey-Babe," joked Buzooms. "But she's right, some women don't like being called Darling or Babe by a stranger."

Mouse Girl added, "So, Will, what I hear you saying is that you're fine with ignoring the last ten years of progress women have made in terms of—"

Will interrupted, "Yeah—in terms of feminist bullshit. See, I don't buy all that 'I'm soooo oppressed' crap."

"I'll be back in a minute," said the waitress, discreetly walking away.

Five minutes later it was all forgotten—or so I thought. The next night we were eating in a Cuban restaurant, "La Rosa." As we seated ourselves in a semi-circular booth, Will and Mouse Girl slid in from opposite ends hoping to avoid each other, but ended up sitting side by side in the middle. Mouse Girl ordered *ropa vieja* with yellow rice, plantains, and extra bread.

"That's a big plate of food, *Señora*. You might want to split that with your boyfriend there," cautioned the waitress, looking at Will.

Mouse Girl, with a look of revulsion, tried to create space from Will and said, "I'll be fine. Thank you. And he is certainly NOT my boyfriend."

Dale Dapkins

The mediation course progressed steadily, and all too soon it was our last day. Mrs. Tupper let us role-play all that afternoon while she consulted her phone. We ended the day with Mrs. Tupper assigning role-play parts to three of us.

"I want Mouse Girl to play a newly hired teacher who is suing her school district because she felt harassed and was subsequently fired for unfair accusations by the school board and their representative. Will, you'll be that representative. Unfortunately, you were trained only in budgetary concerns, not disciplinary policy. Because the principal is on leave, they assigned you the unpleasant task of 'Having a little talk' with Mouse Girl. You resent having to do the principal's job, for which you have no training or experience. Dale, you will play the mediator handling this case."

Mouse Girl, Will, and I walked to the front and sat facing the class. After I gave the introduction of the process we would follow, I asked Mouse Girl if she would please state, in her own words, what led her to seek mediation.

She began, "I had taken this new job teaching English at Key West High School, and I thought I was doing a pretty good job. That day, I was in my classroom correcting papers when Mr. Will Rogers, here, knocked and came in. He appeared nervous, sweaty. He had perspiration stains under his arms."

Will glared at her.

"Anyway, he asked if we could talk for a minute. I said, sure, and he started out saying that he and the other teachers just wanted to get to know me better; they wanted to learn more about my teaching methods—something like that. I told him I grew up in Elkhart, Indiana. I'm a single mom, I enjoy walking and riding my bicycle, and I'm looking to join a choir that sings gospel.

He said the usual pleasantries and that he would pass that information along, and then he asked, "Any problems—any issues?"

At this point—and it happened so seamlessly I almost didn't realize they'd stopped using the past tense recounting their supposed conversation that day and had switched over to present tense. They began having their conversation in real time.

Mouse Girl continued, "Issues? No. Everything's good."

Will said, "And, oh, there's one more thing."

"And what's that?"

"Well, the front office was wondering if y'all were familiar with our rules of discipline. You know, keeping order in your classes."

"I'm aware of the rules."

"I'm sure you are. But these are old-school teachers who just want to maintain their high standard of discipline, that's all. Four of them went to school right here at Key West High."

"You can tell them that I certainly want the same thing."

"And while we're on that subject, they wanted me to inform you that some of your students were reported causing a disturbance—a ruckus, when coming out of y'all's class."

"My class? Really?"

"Hey, don't shoot me, I'm just the messenger."

"Okay, well maybe some of the kids get excited by material that we're covering. But a ruckus? I guess it's hard for people sitting all day in glass offices to tell the difference between enthusiasm and a 'ruckus.' But I can assure you that it's just harmless enthusiasm."

"Oh, and one more thing."

"And what might that be?"

Dale Dapkins

"I—they were wondering if you're aware of complaints by two girls in your English class that some of the boys were taking sexual liberties with them?"

Will and Mouse Girl seemed to be ad-libbing their own soap opera. I glanced at Mrs. Tupper who was on her phone. I turned back as Mouse Girl said, "I think the school rules on social behavior are pretty clear. And I'm telling you and your Bible-thumper bureaucrats that these are good kids who follow the rules. None of the girls, or the boys for that matter, have complained about sexual harassment. But I can assure you that if they do, I will certainly let you know."

"See, the thing is—we have a committee for handling these kinds of things proactively here."

"Where you try to hush things up?"

"C'mon now. Not hushing anything up. We just want to head off any problems before they become, you know, public issues."

"No, I don't know. It sounds to me like you're trying to censor. And, the way I hear it, ever since a certain group of prissy ladies got elected to your school board, they've been exercising their own evangelical brand of moral judgment. And that it was these people, AND YOU, who got Principal Philips fired on what everyone I talk to, says was for 'wokeness?' Whatever the Hell that is."

"Y'all best be careful, little girl. Y'all don't wanna go down that rabbit hole."

I stood up and said, "Okay, let's everybody take a step back now. Can we?"

Will and Mouse Girl looked at me like I was some nineteenth century British outsider wearing a pith helmet entering their indigenous village in the middle of a very sacred Oompa Boompa ritual.

The Great Mediator

Will seemed to snap out of it, and addressed me and the whole group, "Can't y'all please tell her that we're just role-playing here?"

Before anyone could respond, Mouse Girl said to Will, "So, let me get this straight; what I hear you saying is that some idiot do-gooders think I have moral issues? I know this is supposed to be play acting, but your tone of voice, Will, is insulting. And I resent having to defend myself against your misogynist Rick Santorum cowboy low-life bullshit."

Will said, "How did we get from what some role-playin, crazy-lady teacher with librel social norms believes to attacking my personal views on women? Hey! I love women. I'm their biggest fan."

Mouse Girl balled her fists and said, "Your stupid claptrap is making me sick. What I'm hearing 'y'all' implying is that I and this fictitious morally questionable crazy teacher-lady from the sinful North, is trying to brain-wash students with racy sex-ed books?"

"Honestly, I don't know what y'all're talking about."

"So, you never heard of Critical Race Theory?"

"Well, yeah, But I admit I don't really get into that stuff. I don't even understand y'all's Critical Race Theory, but listen, I'm just trying to..."

Will was rattled. I considered ending the exercise, and tried to catch Mrs. Tupper's eye, but couldn't. Was she ignoring me?

Will was saying, "You know, y'all Northerners got different views from us down here in Florida on sex education, abortion, voter fraud, all these things that're driving America back into an age of librel darkness. By the way, I'm not the enemy here. No way. Not my style. But they picked me. So here I am."

(Will was back playing his role as the high school administrator.)

"Somebody in the front office knowd Rodeo Will'd be the kind-a guy who'd stand up for Southern values. And because everybody thinks Ol' Rodeo-Will can handle fast-talkin' skinny-ass ladies."

This was the first time I'd heard Will refer to himself as Ol' Rodeo Will, someone from a different life— a different planet. I am suspicious of people who refer to themselves in the third person as if they're able to divide into two selves, one of which can stand apart praising the other part. I'm sorry but I see this as a serious form of mental illness.

Mouse Girl responded.

"What I'm hearing from you sir, is a bunch of frightened, nutso, man-splainin' ideas about women."

I said, "Can we just calm down?"

Mouse Girl turned on me, "Why don't you just shut up, Dale, and keep your whiney opinion to yourself?"

Turning back to Will she said, "I'm sick of guys like you getting your macho jollies playing some cow-punching brain-dead puppet soldier for the Republican war on women. You're like the Taliban!"

I tried to parody our class, "Sooooo, Mouse Girl, what I hear you saying is that—"

But she cut me off. "What part of 'Stay the fuck out of this' don't you understand, Dale?"

I stammered, "Hey, I just..."

Will said, "Look, Doll, y'all might not believe this, but we might be on the same side."

This was so absurd that I, Mouse Girl, and everyone in the room stared at Will.

Mouse Girl's slender body started to shake.

I asked her if she was all right and if she wanted to continue. Spraying thick droplets out her nose, she barked, "Just because this idiot here snorts nasty shit out his horse's ass, you both think I'm gonna go hide like some wimpy little mouse? You don't know who you're dealing with! Listen, I can handle anything that small-minded people like you throw at me. I've been doing it all my life—getting back up after being knocked down—humiliated. Well, guess what? I don't take that shit anymore."

Will approached her. "Hey—c'mon, we all just play-acting, right? I thought—"

He reached out to hug Mouse Girl, but she pushed him away violently. Will and I both turned toward Mrs. Tupper who was still on her phone. She waved the back of her hand at us indicating we should go on.

Will turned to face the class asking "Did I do something wrong here? I mean I just..."

That's when Big Foot approached Mouse Girl and wrapped her strong arms around her shuddering body. And before I could stop her, Buzooms swallowed me like a Dune sandworm. Everyone hugged.

Mrs. Tupper came up and folded Will in her arms announcing, "Okay, I guess that's it for this group. I want to congratulate each and every one of you on your zeal and enthusiasm. If anybody needs help processing any of this, you can always call me."

She wrote an 800 number on the board. Only later did I realize it was 1-800-EAT-SHIT.

I took the bus back to Key West and walked home from the station out by the airport. Turning the corner on my street I saw a crowd gathered in front of Dave's place with him sitting behind a table. Behind him a hand-scrawled sign read "YARD SALE."

"What's all this?" I asked, standing beside a lady buying an armful of parrot print shorts.

Dale Dapkins

"Two dollars for everything," said Dave before he saw me, then, "Jesus Christ, look what the cat just dragged in."

"What happened, man?"

"I got sucker-punched by the Feds—took me for everything. Mom kept houndin' me to put the house in her name, not my law firm's. They took my house, man. Bank accounts froze. Credit card kaput. Said I been lawyering without a license. Tax shit. Said I didn't file for last twelve years. Now they're snooping into everything. I mean everything! Dale, youse might as well know, Dave's not my real name. Enough about me. What about youse? How'd yer thing go? Hey, I should'a told youse before, but I never took that mediation course. The old lady, she kicked me out the first day."

Sometime in the next week, Dave, his mom, and Stinky left after midnight. No forwarding address. No goodbye. Just *pffft*. He did leave me his gold crucifix necklace in my mailbox. It's not real gold. His note read, "For the next great mediator."

But I never became a great mediator. Instead, I became a Head Start teacher. Three to five-year-olds. Must be potty trained. Right! Anyway, my mediation skills work great on kids.

BTW, Bigfoot emailed me saying Will and Mouse Girl got married and had a baby girl. Dolly.

A Tough House to Sell

by ML Condike

"There's a woman in the lobby who wants to list a property."

"Where is it?" Lola, the office real estate broker asked.

Her assistant shrugged. "No idea. But apparently, her mother died there. She doesn't want it. Called it a dog."

"Bring her up. I'll get the details." Lola didn't get to where she was by refusing a few dogs. She could move any property.

At the staff meeting the next morning Lola showed the team her new listing. "It's an older home on No Name Key. The owner died and her daughter's selling it."

Pete, her most-senior agent, laughed. "Good luck. Besides being a fixer-upper, it has a stigma."

"What do you mean?" rookie agent Sandy asked.

Lola sighed. "He means the last three owners died in the house. But I'm not worried. They lived there a long time and just grew old."

"I'm telling you. It won't sell. It's more than just a dog." Pete's eyebrows raised. "It needs an exorcist. I have a friend..."

Lola waved her hand. "Just a bunch of rumors."

***

"What now?" Lola's assistant asked.

"Have the house painted. Empty it out, then have Brad from Royal Furniture stage it." Lola smiled. "Then invite the team to a private showing. And order coffee and donuts."

***

"Gorgeous...charming." The agents couldn't say enough about how Lola had improved the place. Lola's ambition rubbed off on all her agents and attracted the real go-getters.

"I've got just the buyer." Pete's greedy eyes scanned the interior. "I'll call them right now. Maybe they're available this afternoon."

"I've got someone, too," Sandy said.

Pete stepped forward. "Me first! I've got seniority."

Lola laughed. "Calm down. But both of you can show it. A little competition might boost the sale price."

Sandy scowled. "All right."

***

"This is it." Pete said as he pulled into the driveway. He could tell by the couple's reaction Lola's efforts with the house had improved its curb appeal.

Pete unlocked the front door, then swung it open. "You first."

The wife stepped into the foyer followed by her husband.

"Oh my. You can't be serious," the woman said.

Pete stuck his head in and looked around. An unmade bed blocked the foyer. The kitchen and living room furniture had been swapped. The living room drapes lay under the coffee table where the rug had been. The refrigerator stood in the dining room.

A Tough House to Sell

"I have no idea what happened." Pete shuddered. He had a bad feeling. "Someone must have broken in."

"Forget it," the husband said. "Let's visit the next house. This neighborhood isn't for us."

***

Once back at the office Pete told Lola. "Shouldn't you call the police?"

"No. I'll have Brad restage it. My assistant can get the locks changed. Somebody must have a key. A neighbor. Or one of the cleaning crew." Lola thought for a moment. "Way too much effort for it to be a neighborhood prank. Probably wasn't a neighbor."

"It's definitely a puzzler." Still uneasy, Pete rubbed his chin.

***

Lola had the creepy house on No Name Key restaged and fitted with new locks in time for the weekend showings. The listing photos had attracted a half-dozen potential buyers.

Lola had the first appointment on Saturday morning with an older couple from New Jersey. The wife babbled on about moving south.

"We can't stand the winters," the husband added as they approached the house.

Lola unlocked the door and checked the foyer. Everything looked okay, but to be sure, she decided to enter alone first. "Wait here while I turn on the lights."

As soon as she stepped inside, Lola felt a presence. Then she spotted an open *OurKeyWest* magazine floating over the couch, hovering like a drone. The TV flicked on. A black and white shot of an old hotel flashed across the screen. Then creepy music played as a familiar looking guy wearing a wig and women's clothing climbed the stairs.

"Omigod!" Turning around, Lola rushed out. Badly shaken, but determined to make a sale, she said, "Better skip this house. The cleaning crew missed it. Let's visit the property on Big Pine Key."

***

Back at the office, Lola barged into Pete's office. "You're right. That property on No Name...it's haunted. I still can't believe what happened. I couldn't show it." She told him about the floating magazine and the TV.

"What'd I tell you? A stigma!"

"And maybe a ghost! Who owned that property?" Lola retrieved the historical tax records. "Robert A. Bloch briefly owned it in 1958."

Pete's eyes widened. "The guy wrote *Psycho*. Certainly, you've heard of that story."

Lola wasn't about to give up. She paced the room deep in thought. "Maybe if I...No that won't work! But I could..."

"Could what?" Pete asked.

She didn't reply.

"You're never going to sell it."

"I've never met a house I couldn't sell."

"You've never met one like this house," Pete said.

Facing Pete with her jaw firmly set, Lola asked, "What's the name of that exorcist you know?"

Florida is Fake Fruit

by Mia Shawn

Her love for Mickey morose,
poisonous politicos coast to coast.
Her caring is moot,
Florida is Fake Fruit.

Tilting with Storm gods June to December.
Starving manatees' seagrass only to remember.
Sugar fields smoke skyward, incinerated shoots.
Florida is Fake Fruit.

Her Coral Reef's health is history.
Her water quality monitoring a mystery.
Her culprits? Fulminant fertilizer and people poop.
Florida is Fake Fruit.

Climate chaos will cultivate change.
Florida's human priorities soon rearranged.
Her fecund Legacy and Paradise to recoup.
Drifting down in saline seas, sink
Florida's Fake Fruits.

Sign from the Sea

by Patty Tiffany

"You know I'm afraid of water. And I hate hot sand." Phil had always loved the ocean but dreaded its power. He knew every water legend and sea monster from the Sirens of the Rhine to the location of Atlantis, and I had listened to those tall tales long into many nights. He seemed obsessed with them now that we lived on an island.

"Of course, but we're close to the bathhouse. We can wade a bit at least." I knew all his phobias, some I enjoyed, some I had given up on.

"Wading can lead to swimming, Joycie." He liked to use his pet name for me to be persuasive. He'd blink those scoundrel eyes of his for emphasis when he really wanted something.

My frail of form, funny, brainy Phil, the only Navy guy I ever knew who couldn't swim very well. And here I was visiting on his first assignment to Boca Chica in Key West, both testing the chance of rekindling old feelings. And succeeding. It had been a great few weeks, wandering the quirky town, dodging tourist hangouts, and watching huge yachts arriving in the bight. Making love like newlyweds.

I was determined to get past at least one of his phobias—the water looked like a postcard from paradise, and he was going in. "Just a few steps, Sweets," I said. "Let's just try it."

He put a careful toe in and looked at me with fear.

Sign from the Sea

"Don't you feel that?

"Warm water, yes."

"No, the attaching. Something is attaching to me."

"Imagination more like it. Nothing is attaching to us. Go in with me, I mean it."

He moved a few footsteps beside me, his feet like weights.

I took his hand, and he jumped back.

"Can't you feel the water pulling you? It's like a bite with venom pouring through me." He was always coming up with weird notions. To him, the sand, the water, the wind—were alive.

Lead by example, I thought, and jumped in ahead of him like a small tarpon surfacing and looking back.

But he stood frozen. Feet firm on the seashell-white sand and not one move toward me.

I paddled and encouraged, splashing my come-ons. "The water's perfect!" I turned to shout.

It took a moment as my eyes scanned the beach and palm trees. He was gone.

Nothing left but his towel.

I power swam back and ran to the towel. No sign.

I looked down again, and the towel was gone.

No matter how scared, he can't move that fast. Maybe the bathhouse?

So I ran there, gulping the thick air.

"Phil," I cried at the curved wall entrance.

"No," he screamed. A no of horror and fascination.

I turned into the dark corner. "Phil, where are you?"

Now a calmer, deeper voice said, "Don't worry, we're working."

"Working on what? Who's we?"

"I'm with Neptune now...his spirit and I are forming a new plan for the planet."

184

"Phil, I'm scared. I can't see you."

"You don't have to see me. Just wait."

And I stood, swaying in the hot Keys' air, my wet bathing suit feeling like a vise.

When he came out of the shadows, I stopped breathing.

"Phil?"

"No, not now. We are one, Neptune and I have made decisions."

I could see new sinewy muscle, laces of seaweed, a new dark profile, and a trident. A fierceness flowed from him I had never known.

"Behind this wall, the water printer of our new plan will show the people what must happen. Word will spread...humans love signs, and they may listen to this one."

"But, Phil, why you?" I began as he interrupted.

"I must leave now, my Darling Joyce. There is much to organize. Humans will have a choice. If they allow sea creatures to rule, the peace of our world may come to them. If not, well... You may come with me now, if you want this new life."

"But are you sure someone will share the plan?" A few weeks of our bliss was flashing brightly in my mind, even as I feared this sudden new creature, ruler of seas like the legends he treasured.

"If not someone, then a creature from my kingdom. The dolphin receive all my messages. They can translate."

He extended his hand, now like a webbed fin.

I reached out, then hesitated, my body trembling. Leaving everything for him? Then he fixed his newly greenish eyes on me, an ultimatum of love and protection.

Sign from the Sea

"Now." His words chiseled the air between us. "You must decide."

As I touched him, his love came at us like a tidal wave, and we surged forward with fins for feet. I felt my teeth go to tiny spikes and my back popping new scales as we were washed forward.

"But what about the printer and the plan?" I asked, many years later darting after him along the deep ledges of the Pacific.

"I wanted you with me. I changed my mind about the walkers on land—they're not worth saving."

If Only...

by Joanna Gray

A pril on the Jersey Shore. Icy, gray days slumped into dark nights. No fishing. There were fish, of course. Flounder were running, some early blues, but with the wind and sleet? Even the most intrepid fishermen were home. Sure, I toughed it out on the beach a couple times this spring. All I got was wind burned and more depressed.

Our house. A newly built, beautiful, three-story F-you to Hurricane Sandy. After the storm, we went fifteen-rounds with fate and the Feds. Lawyers and endless paperwork. Shifting state guidelines. Contractors and elusive permits. A diminished retirement to cover costs. An initial Rocky-style loss followed by a Rocky II victory. The fight to rebuild had occupied us for three years. Now, all we had was the grind. And cold, damp wind.

Light from the windows highlighted gaping, empty planters and the Japanese maple that didn't make the winter. My used-to-be-a-runner-but-now-unmotivated wife on the couch, staring at HGTV. She hadn't showered. I knew I was struggling, but to not shower? That was just giving up.

Look, I get it. As a beer salesman, I spent my days hitting one dingy dive liquor store after another, groveling for placements, eating my pride for lunch to make quotas. We had the mortgage on a house that no longer existed, and the loan needed to finish this one. We would never, ever, ever see the end of this debt. But, hell, I still showered.

What had become of us? We had dreams once: Palm trees and warm sun. A charter boat. The book *How to Quit Your Job and Move to Key West* lay on the coffee table, mocking. Our last trip there, only a month ago, dulled from memory by dim winter sun. Numbed by unfulfilled promises of an early spring. Damn you Punxsutawney Phil.

I flopped in the chair. Not too close—if she smelled, I didn't want to know. I still wore my winter coat. My winter coat. In April.

"You have your coat on."

"So?"

"It's wet. It'll ruin the fabric. That was paperwork round number sixteen that got us that chair. It's precious." Her deadpan said otherwise. I picked up the book.

"Remember the first time you came to Key West with me?"

She brightened. "Yeah, we were still on the tarmac, and I said, 'Why aren't we living here?'"

"You had to take sick days to get the time off. Had to stay out of the sun."

"Ha! That was impossible! And it was February." She sat up, warming to the memory. "I was hoping I'd get caught and fired. Then I wouldn't have to leave. The vibe of the town, the people. The palm trees!"

"And a decent glass of wine in almost every bar," I reminded her.

"Ahh… that's culture," she laughed. I missed that laugh.

"Jo." I became all business. "I can't do this anymore. I'm going to quit my job. We're moving to Key West."

"Ok."

She sobered, lay back down. She knew, like me, that it was an empty promise. Too much invested here. Too hard to change.

It'll happen, I promised myself. It'll happen.

A month went by. A month of taking orders, taking shit, taking Xanax. Defiant Hawaiian shirts on Fridays, Buffet on the Sirius. Daydreams about "someday…"

Memorial Day weekend. Time to start making money. Tourists returning to the Shore, buying the swill I sell to liquor stores and restaurants. Earning a year's worth of pay in eight vital weekends. Sun was predicted, flowers bloomed. Should be good.

Ah, but nope. Rain. Cold rain. The weekend a complete washout. I watched the streets flood, my bank account drain. Monday was to be a BBQ. Instead, I spent it with bitter liquor store managers trying to return unsold cases and kegs. May quotas went out the window, just like the determination I had in April. Seven weekends to make a year's salary. I knew from experience what a kick in the gut this summer would be. Even when it got warm, this job still sucked.

Home. Maybe I could BBQ in the garage? An image of the house in flames, the insurance adjuster maniacally laughing as Jo and I succumbed to a quicksand of paperwork. I nixed the idea.

Jo was in the office, rain curtaining windows, the room a foggy gloom. She wasn't showered. At this point,

If Only...

I couldn't blame her. Get dressed and do what? At least HGTV wasn't on.

"Whatca doin'?" I asked.

"Not much. Did some grading. Applied for a teaching job in Key West."

"Ok," I said. Though my heart couldn't help skipping a beat. If only...

We both knew the lottery was more likely. A teaching gig was hard to come by. Cutthroat. Based on who you knew or went to school with. Especially a history position. It was a miracle she'd gotten the teaching job she had. Apparently, her principal had thought bartenders with history degrees made good teachers. Managing drunk adults and distracted teenagers was essentially the same thing.

A week later, Jo had a phone interview with someone at Key West High School. Her first interview in fifteen years. She googled trends, practiced, wrote out answers. She even dressed for it.

"If I dress confident, I'll sound confident," she declared as she slipped on a blazer and dress pants. "Besides, when we move, I'm leaving these behind. Right in the closet. A welcome gift to the new owners."

"I'm leaving that winter coat. And my snow boots."

"And sweaters and scarves." We listed items we'd no longer need for a full ten minutes before her call.

Then weeks passed. Nothing. We spent 4th of July by the fire pit, brooding over the missed opportunity. Our wistful "Imagine ifs" of the past month turned into "if onlys."

Imagine fishing all year, imagine biking everywhere, imagine no jug-handles, and making left turns! If only it happened. If only she had gotten the job, we could call Key West home…

We weren't so young and reckless that we'd move without prospects. Actually, Jo would. But for some reason she loved me and wanted me to go with her and I needed prospects. God, I was a stick-in-the-mud.

It was just as well, we reasoned. We'd been back in the house a year. Did we really want to move, again? Our whole life was here. Family, friends. If we needed anything, I knew a guy. My job had some perks. Free beer, for starters.

But still. If only…

Mid July, but I wore a ski cap, gloves, and scarf. A fleece zipped up over a hoodie. The epic ass who ran this particular account made sure it was always my ass frozen in the coolers doing inventory. His store was my strongest numbers, but a man has a breaking point, and I was dangerously close to mine. Would it be a breakdown? Or would I murder this guy? Maybe lock him in the cooler, watch his body slowly shut down, just like my soul.

Wow, that went south real fast. I snapped out of it. South. Key West. If only…

My phone rang. Jo. She usually texted. Someone must have died.

"What's the matter?"

"I got the job."

"What job?"

"*The* job."

"I'm in the cooler. I'll call you back."

The walk to the front of that dingy store was the longest and shortest of my life. Pulse pounding in my ears. I saw the grime and years of neglect in minute detail, the

If Only...

missing point-of-sale on my display, the desperate look of
the kid behind the counter, his shoulders slumped knowing
this was all there was. I saw myself in him and stood
straighter.

"Hey," he called to me. "You were supposed—"

"Not now," I snapped, holding my hand up like a
crossing guard.

Pushing through the door, I knew I had just stepped
out of my old life and into my new. I stood in the parking
lot, taking in the moment, then called Jo.

"So..."

"Ninth grade history." Her voice quivered.

"That's awesome! That's what you wanted!"
Silence. "What?" My gut wrenched, waiting for the catch.
I looked around; was I being punked?

"There's a catch."

"I gathered that. Just spit it out."

"I start in three weeks. We have to quit everything
we've ever known in three weeks. Sell the house, say
goodbye. *Find* a house. In three weeks."

My first reaction was no. Impossible. Too risky.
Too much. Then a memory. Memories: Fishing the pier,
invited by strangers to join a bocce game, Boat House
happy hours. Art markets and street fairs. Characters
everywhere, both obvious and subtle. It felt like home. It
was home. We knew our town, loved our house, but
something about Key West fit. Or rather, as we would
come to realize, we fit Key West.

"Even so," she said, breaking my reverie. "I think I
should take it. I'm taking it. We're going." Her voice
unsteady. Joy, disbelief, fear.

"Yes." I was physically incapable of saying anything more. Joy, disbelief, fear.

"Russ, we are quitting our jobs and *moving to Key West!*"

We both laughed, giddy like Christmas morning.

There was a long pause. "Russ?"

"Yeah?"

"Now what?"

The author— who is, in fact, Jo— and her husband, have called Key West home for over five years. They fish and bike and do not own winter coats. And yes, they still have their copy of *Quit Your Job and Move to Key West*. They highly recommend it.

The Ridiculous Truth About the Scrumptious Snail: A Poem

by Judi D. Winters

Madame Escargot's pheromones raged,
at a snail's pace.
"*C'est ridicule,*" rasped Monsieur,
whose visceral hump always screamed for more.

"A free-wheelin' conch I'm not," she yelped,
"Unlike my cousin, the whimpering whelk."
Monsieur excreted comeuppance.
"*Bien sur, vous n'êtes pas, Madame!*
(of course, you're not, Madame!)
"You, my escargot, are a slug!"

Her femininity insulted, Madame flipped over,
clammed her foot, head, neck, and tail beneath
her sheath,
vociferously declaring,
"*Pas ce soir, pas ce soir Joseph!*"
(Not tonight, not tonight, Joseph!)

Judy D. Winters

Concatenating, they spiraled,
riding the king tide through deadened mimosa
leaves.
To Cayo Hueso's blackened watery depths, they
plunged.
Madame, a nervously grousing limpet, pedal-
waved first.
Monsieur, a scoundrel at heart, passionately
pursued.

Sliming homeward,
they salsaed to the bight's sandy bed.
She skipped agin her slippered shell, and
juddered, alone.
Retreating to dreams alive in the darkness,
silent murmurings of mysterious anonymous sex.

Monsieur's amorous tintinnabulations
and soulful music implored,
*"Mais, mon Cherie, maintenant. Maintenant,
mon Cherie?"*
(But my love, now. Now my love?)
Madame's reverie broke,
freeing a refrained frisson of desire.

She manically crawled closer and feigned a
salutary kiss.
*"Peut-etrê, peut-etrê demain soir, Joseph, mon
amour!"*
(Perhaps, perhaps tomorrow night, Joseph, my
love!)
His hope, a complexity of confusion and climactic
renewal.
Tomorrow never came.

The Ridiculous Truth About the Scrumptious Snail: A Poem

Monsieur, the weaker of the two, had a premature
demise.
His skeletal remains crumbled to a salty grave.
Sketched in the sand, Monsieur Mollusque's
obituary read:
"To a hermaphroditic finale"
Oui, Joseph, ce soir, ce soir!
(Yes, Joseph, tonight, tonight!)

Discovery

by BJ Condike

I always thought where I was would help me discover who I am. To learn more about myself I gravitated toward extreme locations—the farthest east, the farthest west, the farthest north, the farthest south.

That September I was as far south as I could get without a passport. The Paradise Bar & Grille was more crowded than it should have been in the slow season. I nursed a beer at a small table and waited for the musicians to set up. I almost walked out when my waitress Tammy said it was a ukulele band. I made a face, but she told me to wait and see, they weren't what you might expect.

I expected music from Don Ho or Tiny Tim, or tunes from the ubiquitous Jimmy Buffett, which were a staple in many Key West bars.

What Rocky Beach and His Ukaholics delivered were tunes from Merle Haggard, Johnny Cash, and the elder Hank Williams. The quartet lacked a steel guitar, but the ukes did a fine job with the music, and the vocals weren't bad either. There was none of that New Country pablum that made me feel like that time I threw up in middle school.

At one point a lanky, thirty-something brunette sauntered in and surveyed the room. All the tables but mine were occupied by parties of two or more.

She shouted at me over the din, "May I sit here?"

Discovery

She was casually dressed in a crop top, short-shorts, and strappy sandals. I didn't particularly want her company, but I didn't want to be rude, either. I waved an assent and yelled back, "Sure!"

She pulled up a chair and instantly Tammy appeared. Unasked, she placed a drink in front of my new tablemate, a blue concoction that looked like Tidy Bowl over ice with a sprig of mint. The brown-haired woman took a sip and said something to the waitress about the mix being off. Tammy nodded and trotted away.

The brunette opened a book, laid it on the table, and began to read, apparently not interested in me or the music.

Once the Ukaholics concluded their set, Tammy reappeared and I ordered another beer. I asked the book reader if I could buy her a drink. Sometimes I can't help myself.

She raised her half-filled tumbler and said, "Got one, thanks," with a deprecating look.

Having already sacrificed my private table, I ignored the look. "But I heard you say that the mix was bad. Wouldn't you like a new drink more to your liking?"

She half-smiled and shook her head. "No, I said the mix on the band's music was bad—too much volume in the drums and not enough in the vocals." She waved off the waitress. "It's okay, Tammy. I'm good." She went back to her book.

I had nothing to do until the beer arrived, so I peeked at the book.

"What are you reading?"

Without replying, the brunette turned the book so I could read the jacket and kept reading.

"*Ain't Nobody Nobody*," I read out loud. "Any good?"

The brunette sighed, slowly inserted a bookmark, and closed it like it was a rare first edition. She clasped her hands over it and took a breath.

"It's pretty good," she said, "for a debut novel, even if the title is a double-negative."

"Who's Heather Harper Ellett?"

"I don't know. Like I said, it's her first book. The plot's a bit tortuous, but her writing is clean. She uses too many figures of speech for my taste, but it's quite readable."

"What are you, a book critic?"

"No, I just like to read, which is why I'm here." She reached for her book.

I persisted. "But why here? In a bar? With live music, no less."

"I read to escape."

"Escape what?"

"This..." She gestured at our surroundings. "Paradise." She opened her book. "Besides, I've heard the Ukaholics before."

"Are you a groupie? You follow them, but you don't like them?"

She closed the book with a thump. "No, I do like them."

"They must know you. Enough so they listen when you tell them their sound mix is off."

"Of course they know me. Rocky's my brother."

"Oh." I grinned "Well, hello, Rocky's sister." I extended my hand. "I'm Vince. Vince Ricci."

She made no move to accept my greeting. "That's too bad."

"What's so bad about it?"

"My father told me to never trust a man with two first names. Vince. Ritchie."

"It's spelled R-I-C-C-I, not R-I-T-C-H-I-E."

Discovery

She nodded and pursed her lips. "Okay. You're forgiven, but just this once."

"So...I'm Vince. And you are...?"

"Sorry. I'm Sandy."

I raised my eyebrows. "If you're Rocky's sister, does that make you...?"

She grimaced. "I know. Sandy Beach."

"My turn to be sorry."

She shrugged. "My parents thought they were funny."

"Were they Beach Boys fans or something?"

"Look, I don't know you well enough for this conversation." She drained the rest of her blue cocktail. "So, Vince R-I-C-C-I, what about that drink?"

I had bantered myself into a corner like a Bedard duck.

"Sorry." I shook my head "That was a limited offer. I was just being polite. I can barely afford beer." I raised my half-empty glass to prove it.

"More's the pity." She studied me through squinted eyes. "Have you been here before?"

"No, I'm new in town," I said. "And you could use a new line."

"That wasn't a line, and you're not that new. I saw you over at Sloppy Joe's last week. You looked lonely."

"I am not lonely. I'm alone. There's a difference. I'm exploring the town by myself. I'm surprised you noticed me."

"You have a memorable face. Anyone ever tell you that you look like Tom Selleck?"

"Ah—the old, 'You look like a movie star' line," I said. "Next you'll be asking me up to see your etchings. You do need some new material."

BJ Condike

"I don't have any etchings," she quipped, "and if I did, I wouldn't show them to you. And my material works just fine, thanks."

"No offense, okay? You're an attractive woman, but I'm just not..."

There was an awkward pause, interrupted by Tammy bringing me my beer, and a new Tidy Bowl drink for Sandy. I hadn't seen Sandy ask for a refill. They exchanged looks but not words.

I wanted to make amends, so I changed topics. "So what are you doing at other clubs? Reading? You weren't following the Ukaholics because they weren't at Sloppy Joe's."

"Checking out the competition."

"I don't understand."

"Other clubs," she said. "I own this one."

"Ah! That explains it."

"Explains what?"

"Why Tammy keeps bringing you drinks unasked. She's kissing up to the boss."

"Never mind her," she said. "What do you do?"

"I'm a writer."

"Oh, God. Another Hemingway wannabe. He-man and all."

"I'm not a he-man."

"So—what—you have a cat?" She adopted a mock-horrified look. "Don't tell me you have one of Hemingway's cats—the ones with six toes?"

"No! I'm not a Hemingway fan. I'm more of an aspiring Thomas Williams."

"Now I don't understand."

"You know, 'A Streetcar Named Desire?' 'Cat on a Hot Tin Roof?'"

201

"There's that cat theme again. And you mean Tennessee Williams." Her eyes grew wide. "Oh! Wait. Cats. Not a he-man. I'm sorry. I'm so dense."

I welcomed her epiphany. Not that I was as definite about myself as she was, but it cleared the air. "His given name was Thomas. His mother called him Tom."

She recovered. "That's right. I'd forgotten."

"Most people don't know that—but you knew about Hemingway's cats."

"I live here, remember? Both men lived in Key West at one time or another. There are museums for them in town. You should visit them. You might connect with their muses."

"I've already been, and I have my own muse, thanks."

"And who might that be?"

"It's Samuel—"

Tammy interrupted my reply when she reappeared and whispered in Sandy's ear.

"Excuse me," Sandy said as she stood. "Something needs my attention. Nice meeting you, Vince R-I-C-C-I." She murmured something to Tammy. "And the beers are on the house."

I nodded a thank-you with a smile and watched her weave her way toward the bar.

I left soon after and returned to my room and my laptop. The play wasn't going to write itself.

***

I stared at the screen and began to type:

ACT II
Scene 1

The curtain opens on a dimly lit living room. There is a closed door stage right and an open door stage left. In center stage are a small couch with matching end tables and lamps. A quilt is draped over the back of the couch. Streetlight shines from an upstage window onto the furniture.

Impatient knocking is heard stage right, followed by a doorknob rattle and the click of a deadbolt. A thirty-something TOMMY staggers into the room holding a large key fob. He's dressed in jeans and a flannel shirt.

TOMMY. Mona? Mona! (TOMMY stumbles into the couch, then bumps into an end table and knocks over a lamp.)

TOMMY. Aw, shit!

(CHERYL enters stage left and flicks the wall switch, lighting the stage. She is Tommy's age and attractive, barefoot and wearing a nightshirt. She squints and brushes disheveled hair from her eyes.)

CHERYL. Tommy? Goddammit, Tommy, what are you doing here? It's the middle of the night!

TOMMY. Lookin' for Mona. Where's Mona?

CHERYL. (walking toward him) You can't barge in like this! You're not supposed to be here.

TOMMY. 'S my house. (He waves his key at her with a smirk and plops onto the couch.)

CHERYL. No, it isn't. Not anymore. (CHERYL reaches for the key, but TOMMY pulls it away.) The judge gave it to me.

TOMMY. Judge was an asshole. Where's Mona? I wanna see my little girl.

Discovery

CHERYL. (taking a deep breath) Ramona's gone, Tommy. You know that.

TOMMY. Gone where?

RALPH. (from offstage left) Cheryl? Are you okay? What's going on?

CHERYL. (yelling over her shoulder, keeping her eye on TOMMY) It's nothing Ralph! I'll handle it.

Ralph enters stage left wearing only boxer shorts. He is forty-ish and out of shape with a paunch.

RALPH. What the hell is he doing here?

CHERYL. I don't know! He's drunk and confused. (CHERYL picks up the lamp.)

RALPH. You want me to throw him out?

CHERYL. Yeah, right. You and who's army?

RALPH. Well—then I'll call the cops.

CHERYL. No, you won't! Just go back to bed. I said I'd handle it.

RALPH. I don't like him here.

CHERYL. Ralph!

RALPH. Okay, okay. (RALPH exits left, slamming the door behind him.)

During the exchange between CHERYL and RALPH, TOMMY'S head droops onto his chest. The noise of the door closing wakes him up.

TOMMY. (looks around) I wanna see Mona.

CHERYL. Ramona's gone, Tommy. She died, remember? The virus? The hospital? The funeral? Tommy? Tommy!

TOMMY. (Beat. TOMMY screws up his face and begins to sob.) No! Not Mona! She's gone, isn't she? My little Mona!

CHERYL. Tommy...

TOMMY. (still weeping) I killed her, didn't I? That's what I did—I killed her!

CHERYL. You don't know that, Tommy.

TOMMY. But I brought it home! The virus! I brought it home and infected her!

CHERYL. Tommy...

TOMMY. I didn't get the shot. I thought it was a hoax. I thought it was like the flu.

CHERYL. We've been through this. It's been over a year. You have to stop obsessing. Are you still seeing Dr. Roberts?

TOMMY. Roberts is an asshole.

CHERYL. The judge is an asshole. Roberts is an asshole. Is everyone an asshole?

TOMMY. All shrinks are assholes. They think they can solve your problems by talking. (TOMMY's manner changes from belligerent to apologetic). I'm so sorry, Cheryl. Can you ever forgive me? Honey?

(CHERYL is standing directly in front of him. As he apologizes, he leans forward and rubs her leg with one hand. She ignores the gesture.)

TOMMY. Can't we make up and be like before? We could—you know—right here, for old times' sake—see where it takes us. (TOMMY reaches out with his other hand.)

CHERYL. (Slaps TOMMY's hand away and steps back.) Now who's the asshole? What in God's name is the matter with you? After all we've been through, you think I'd take you back? I tried to get you vaccinated! But you wouldn't listen! (She turns away and paces the room.) What the hell do I know, anyway? I'm just a nurse. You and your goddamn anti-vax, high-school-dropout buddies at the shop thought you knew better. And now Ramona's dead. Gone forever! And, don't forget, our marriage died long before Ramona did, remember? There was that small, insignificant thing called your boyfriend—what was his name— Francisco? Federico? How do you think that made me feel? Was I not enough for you? Were you always that way? Don't you think you should have told me? What the hell were you... (CHERYL spins around and sees TOMMY passed out, half on and half off the couch. She strides over and shakes him by the shoulders.)

CHERYL. Tommy? Tommy! Wake up and listen to me... (She lightly slaps him on the face a couple of times, but he is unresponsive.) Tommy! (She clenches her fists in frustration.) "Arrrrgh!"

(CHERYL looks at TOMMY and shakes her head. She picks his feet up and crams his legs onto the small couch, covers him with the quilt, and turns to exit stage left. As she reaches the door, she glances back at him.)

CHERYL. Go home, Tommy. Go back to Federico, or whatever his name is. (She flicks off the light and exits, closing door behind her.)

(The stage lights fade to black except for the streetlight from the window shining on Tommy. The sound of the closing door wakes him, and he raises himself up on one elbow.)

TOMMY. Mona? Mona... (He collapses back onto the couch.)

THE CURTAIN FALLS

***

It was the week following Hell Week, that week between Christmas and New Year's when the tourists clogged the roads and crammed the restaurants. The locals grumbled over the traffic snarls, but the hotels and bars needed the income to survive the inevitably quiet off-season.

Sandy strolled up to my table.

"May I join you?" There was no music, and the mid-afternoon crowd was sparse, so she didn't have to shout this time. There were plenty of empty tables.

I grinned. "It's your bar."

Sandy pulled out a chair and sat. She wore a low-cut silky top and mini skirt. "I haven't seen you in a while."

"I've been working."

"Writing?" she said, smiling, "Or honest work?"

"Writing. Isn't that honest work?"

"Only if you get paid. So, how's the novel coming? Are you and Mark Twain communing?"

"Who?"

"The last time we met you said your muse was someone named Samuel. I presumed you meant Samuel Clemens."

I cracked a smile. "You know what they say about assumptions. My muse is Samuel Adams." I lifted my glass in salute to the founding father and famous brew master.

"We don't serve him here."

"So I discovered—but I'm acquiring a taste for your local Iguana Bait brew." To prove it, I sipped some of mine. "And I'm not writing a novel. It's a play. I'm a Tennessee Williams fan, remember?"

"Oh, yes. I remember. More cat-man than he-man."

"I told you I don't own a cat."

"So you say," she said. "Ready to buy me that drink?"

"You do recall I'm not dating women these days."

She nodded. "I know. Not a date—just friends."

"I'm a struggling artist. I can't afford your top shelf spirits, but I'll spring for a beer."

Discovery

"Never mind. I have my standards, and I own the place, remember?"

She caught the eye of a hovering Tammy and gave her a nod. The waitress trotted off to fetch what I presumed would be another one of her blue elixirs.

"Are you seeing anyone?" she asked.

"I'm still working on that."

Sandy shrugged "No worries. This is Key West. We're at the edge of the map. Westernmost island in Florida and southernmost city in the U.S. We're off the beaten path, away from the mainstream. Lots of closet doors open here."

We were drifting into uncomfortable waters. I gave a non-committal shrug.

"So," she said, "what kind of play are you writing? Comedy? Tragedy?"

"At this point it's a drama. Beyond that, I don't know. The way I write it'll probably be a tragedy no matter what."

"Don't be so hard on yourself. I'm sure it'll be great."

"I may never know."

She gave me a quizzical look.

"You can't tell how good a play is until you see it performed on stage. If the director can't visualize it, if the actors can't breathe it, if the audience can't feel it, it's no good."

"So put it on stage."

"It's not that easy," I said. "I need someone to direct it and a theater to produce it."

"There are several theaters here."

"Yeah, but I don't have the connections."

"Well, I know a guy." She gave me a thoughtful look. "You two might hit it off. I'll talk to him and see what he says."

***

ACT III
Scene 1

A barroom. A small table with two chairs. The atmosphere is hazy. Neon beer signs hang on the walls. TOMMY sits at the table with a half-empty whisky glass. A partial pyramid of empty glasses adorns middle of the table.

FEDERICO enters stage left. He's young and athletic. He spies TOMMY and stops, shaking his head. FEDERICO proceeds to the table and sits down. He stares at TOMMY, who ignores him.

FEDERICO. Okay. I'm waiting.

(TOMMY looks at him but does not respond.)

FEDERICO. I want an explanation, Tommy. Where were you all night?

TOMMY. Cheryl's.

FEDERICO. What is it with you and your wife? I told you to stay away from that bitch!

TOMMY. She's my ex-wife!

FEDERICO. I don't care! Christ, you need your head examined. (A thought strikes him.) Omigod! Did you sleep with her?

TOMMY. No! (looking down) Tried, though.

FEDERICO. (shaking his head) This isn't working, Tommy. The drinking, the carousing. You and that...that *puta*!

(TOMMY drains his glass and attempts to balance it on the pyramid. He concentrates but fails and the glasses fall over.)

TOMMY. Cheryl's my wife!

FEDERICO. She's your ex-wife!

Discovery

(TOMMY waves his hand in a vague "whatever" gesture. FEDERICO stands and sweeps the glasses to the floor in a single motion.)

FEDERICO. You're not listening, Tommy! You haven't for a while. I've had it! I'm leaving. I'm going back to New York. You don't care about me. All you care about is your personal problems and I guess I'm not one of them.

(FEDERICO stomps off and exits left. TOMMY folds his arms on the table and buries his head. His shoulders heave with soft sobs.)

THE CURTAIN FALLS

***

I sat at my usual table. Tammy automatically brought me a pint of Iguana Bait in a pilsner glass. I briefly bemoaned my predictability before moistening my mustache with the foamy head.

Sandy arrived a few minutes later. A youngish man tailed behind her dressed in white slacks and an open silk dress shirt

"Vince, this is Pablo. Pablo's the managing director of a local theater. Pablo—Vince, the playwright I told you about."

Pablo and I bumped fists and Sandy left us alone. I warmed up to him when Tammy brought him an amber IPA without asking. I swear that woman is telepathic.

"I read your script," he said, as a means of introduction.

"Don't keep me in suspense."

"I liked it. It's a bit trite with the Covid thing, but not overdone."

BJ Condike

"I don't see how one can avoid it these days. It permeates everything."

"I have some advice on the ending, though, if you're open to it."

"I'm all ears."

"Times being what they are, I'd advise against a tragedy. People have enough of that in their lives. Suicide won't play well with today's audiences. It's too depressing."

"I don't know if I want to change it."

Pablo reached out and placed his hand on my arm. "Please reconsider. These days people need more resurrection and less resignation."

I left his hand where it was.

"Okay. I'll think about it. If I did change it, you think you could get it on stage?"

"I'm sure of it."

***

ACT III
Scene III

A cemetery. A few birds can be heard chirping. CHERYL is on her knees center stage. She places the final touches on a flower arrangement in front of a horizontal headstone. She stands and admires her efforts.

TOMMY enters stage right carrying a small bouquet. He hesitates, then slowly approaches the grave. CHERYL sees TOMMY and takes one or two steps back.

TOMMY. It's okay. I've had my shots. Booster and everything.

CHERYL. (warily) First time I've seen you here.

TOMMY. I had been coming in the mornings, but I'm on day shift now.

Discovery

(TOMMY steps toward the grave.)

TOMMY. It's beautiful here. Ramona would have liked it.

(CHERYL joins him. They both look down at the grave.)

CHERYL. Yes, she would have. It's nice to see you...here. You seem...well.

TOMMY. (shrugs) I've stopped drinking.

CHERYL. Good for you. Are you sleeping?

TOMMY. Yes. And no pills.

CHERYL. Very good. No more ambulance trips to the ER then?

TOMMY. No. Sorry about that. I'm better now.

CHERYL. Are you seeing anyone?

TOMMY. Just Dr. Roberts.

CHERYL. Dr. Roberts the asshole?

TOMMY. (smiles) Yes. But he's not that bad.

CHERYL. Still once-a-week appointments?

TOMMY. Every day, actually.

CHERYL. Every day? Insurance won't pay for that. How can you afford it?

TOMMY. (grins) He doesn't charge me.

CHERYL. Why wouldn't he...? Oh. Oh! Really?

(TOMMY nods.)

CHERYL. Aren't there rules against that?

TOMMY. (shrugs) I don't know. I guess it's ok if it's mutual.

CHERYL. (smiling) Well, I'm happy for you. For you both.

TOMMY. Thanks. How's Ralph?

CHERYL. Oh, he's long gone.

(Awkward silence.)

CHERYL. Well, I've got to get back and feed the dog.

TOMMY. You have a dog?

BJ Condike

CHERYL. Yes. She's a rescue. I decided that's all I can handle. Good-bye, Tommy. Good to see you.

TOMMY. You, too.

(CHERYL exits stage left. TOMMY kneels and places the bouquet on the grave. He rests his hand on the ground and leaves it there for a few seconds. He rises and looks around and nods in satisfaction. TOMMY exits stage right.)

THE CURTAIN FALLS

***

I sat at my usual table with a freshly poured Iguana Bait. Sandy raised her ocean blue cocktail in salute.

"Congratulations, Hemingway!" she said.

"Please, you know I hate that," I said.

"Sorry. Just teasing. I mean congratulations, Tennessee! I hear Pablo's going to direct your play."

"Never compare me to the great Tennessee Williams, but thanks. Yes, I'm going to see it onstage. The rehearsals have helped a lot, and Pablo's been great."

"I hear you're spending a lot of time together."

"Yes, we have been. In fact, we're looking for a place."

Sandy smiled. "Well, I'm happy for you. For you both."

"Thanks. It's been a long time coming."

I always thought where I was would help me discover who I am. I finally realized my true self while living on the Keys' westernmost island, in the country's southernmost city—Key West, Tennessee Williams' second home.

Release

by Rusty Hodgdon

The structure sat askew, permanently tilting to the south. The tires of the double-wide on that side had long since rotted into oblivion. It was in one of the few trailer parks remaining in Key West. The bougainvillea invaded every crack in the dilapidated structure, growing inside like long boney fingers searching for its prey. The brats at school regularly mocked her because of her sordid means.

The four walls were a diabolical prison. She was sent to her room again because of the backtalk. Her boorish, banal parents were quick to banish her with the slightest hint of contrariness. She could try to escape, but that would mean more, and potentially physical, discipline. No, she was trapped. No way out of her mental locks and bars.

She turned the desk chair toward her large, oval, stand-up mirror. At age fifteen, the image that faced her was pleasing. She adored her long, tousled locks, the pert nose and mouth. No blemishes. She was pretty, she thought.

Her thoughts wandered to her class trip to the Key West Butterfly Museum. She was six. This was before her station in life gave rise to the mockery from her classmates. She recalled her utter delight at the sight of thousands of the gentle creatures, their gossamer light blue wings fluttering in the muted light. They alighted upon her by the dozens, their tiny feet tickling her arms and neck.

The next morning, she quietly ate her breakfast and readied herself for school. She answered her mother's inquisitions about her schedule for the day with curt "yes'ms" and "no'ms."

At last, she was out the door. There was something about the morning. A freshness in the air; a slight haze that filtered the sharp edge off the steamy sun.

Two blocks down, she noticed two Monarch butterflies tilting and diving around some peonies along the sidewalk. She was enchanted by their grace, their perseverance. She passed them by, when her progress was halted by a tiny voice, like one that emanated from inside a can. She turned, and not seeing anyone, continued on her way.

Again, she was stopped by the same voice, this time clearer. She could now make out the words.

Priscilla. Priscilla, the voice said. *Come here.*

Startled, she edged closer to the butterflies. The sound was definitely emanating from one of them. Suddenly the butterfly flew up and landed on her shoulder, near her ear.

Priscilla. Come with us. If you dare. The butterfly carried on into the thick bushes. Priscilla followed.

Do you dare? Do you dare? the tiny voice inquired.

Still frightened, she looked at the gentle creature, its gossamer wings beating in the hot air. The fluttering, gentle orange and black colors lured her into an altered state. What if she could follow? Her world suddenly collapsed so she was no more than two inches tall. Her arms became wings. She flew up to a flower petal.

Come with us! Come with us!

Release

She was carried by the thermals and wind, high up, and to the south. She breezed along for hundreds, even thousands of miles, over farms, rivers, mountains, an ocean, stopping only to rest. After a time she could not measure, she landed on a tall, stout tree, with thick convoluted bark. It was in a serene, isolated valley. There she hung, with tens of thousands of her fellow butterflies, and mated, ecstatically.

Not knowing why, it was time to leave, returning the same way, only making stops to mate some more, give birth, and die, a continuous cycle, for eternity.

Storm

by Patty Tiffany

Island oases
where footprints matter
memories on fragile white sand

time measured in shell sounds
seeing you across the bight
billowed roar of a coming storm

swirling your path
a rumble in gray mist
sharpening the water peaks

downward deluge
from blue-gray clouds
stacked beyond heaven

stair steps of rain
flood from sky
wall of water, closer, closer,

as we raise our arms
praise your thunder roll
storm that cracks the sky
come to take us home.

Missing the Boat

by Joanna Brady

Jack's eyes scanned the interior of his boat, moored to the dock along the crowded Key West Marina. He'd laid out all the fixings for girly drinks, like pina coladas, margaritas, or cosmos. Little paper umbrellas—a nice touch—pared lemon rind, a cocktail shaker, his ice bucket. A full bar.

Then carefully—there was nothing haphazard about Jack—he hid the vial of "ruffies" behind the Angostura Bitters.

He checked the restraints he'd installed, then meticulously covered them with a tarp. His sea chest was well-filled with rocks he could use for ballast.

He looked at his watch. Cocktail hour. Perfect. Key West was a great party town. It would be just starting to come alive. It wouldn't take long to find the right girl. He could feel the excitement tingling through his body as he always did. The anticipation, the thrill of the hunt was half the fun.

A glance in the bar mirror told Jack he still had what it took. Humming, he combed his hair one more time, carefully concealing that one shiny spot on his crown. Then he locked up the *Sea Cur* and headed toward shore.

Sea Cur. The name still made him smile. It perfectly suited his predatory proclivities. He'd originally asked for *Sea Dog*, but another boat owner at his yacht club in New Orleans had preempted it. *Sea Cur* was growing on him. It wasn't bad. Suited his wolf-like proclivities. Original. He checked his tourist map and set off for Sloppy Joe's.

He spotted her immediately. She was in her early twenties. A cute redhead; a little on the zaftig side, but not really fat; just sitting there, nursing a cosmo, alone at Sloppy's. A look of sadness dominated her face and there was a weariness in her hazel eyes that signaled vulnerability. Not a barfly, he decided. Certainly not a working girl. It was as though she'd been waiting for him at the bar. This one would be a cinch.

Despite the scattered sprawl of tourists, the bar was relatively quiet. It was early, and the band hadn't yet arrived to drown out conversation.

"On your own?" He pulled up the stool beside her. Not waiting for a reply, he sat down. "May I join you?"

She shrugged.

Keep it light, Jack told himself. Try to avoid clichéd pick-up lines. Friendly. Show empathy. That always works.

"You look like you're ready for another." he said, indicating her drink, now a puddle of melting ice.

"Yeah. Why not? Thanks."

He introduced himself with a phony name. Told her he was a doctor—not mentioning it was in Botany. Her name was Marilyn.

When he asked, "As in Monroe?" she smiled for the first time.

Her smile was ingenuous. Pleasant, showing white, even teeth. Wholesome looking, he thought, with no wild tats or piercings, no goth make-up. She had that air of innocence that he always found charming. He was beginning to like her. He might even keep her alive for a few days. Could be fun.

Missing the Boat

After yet two more drinks, she poured out her litany of miseries. She'd come down to Key West from New Jersey one spring break; loved it and met a guy.

"He managed a dive shop. He was really cute, a nice guy. I fell in love, dropped out of my Physiotherapy course at University of Michigan, and stayed here in Key West. We moved in together, and I thought it might become permanent."

But it was one disappointment after another. First, the guy left for California.

"Tiffany, my next roommate, moved to Austin," she lamented. "I'm working three jobs just to pay the rent. Waitressing, dog-walking, and cooking part-time on boats."

She rolled her eyes. "And that damn hurricane? Irma? A nightmare. I had to evacuate and that took nearly all my savings."

Jack's eyes were glazing over. Enough with the pissing and moaning. She was a chatterbox. Maybe he wouldn't keep her alive very long after all.

The five-piece band arrived on stage and started warming up.

Marilyn looked sidelong at Jack. Not the usual local hitting on me. Seemed like a nice enough guy. A tourist, obviously; early to mid-forties. Good looking. Good quality, casual threads; the boat shoes were new. He's smooth. Well-spoken.

She sighed. "Key West isn't the fun place I thought it would be. I'm moving back to Jersey this summer. I'm gonna go back to school in the fall."

"Back to the grind, huh?" He paused. "Hey, listen, before you do that, how would you like to do something fun? You deserve it, working so hard. Something spontaneous?"

"Like what?"

The musicians were getting louder.

Jack moved in closer, brushing his knee against her thigh, allowing his hand to lightly touch her pinkie finger.

"Like...come away with me for the weekend. I've got a new 38' Island Packet moored at the Key West Marina."

She was impressed. "Wow. That's a great boat. But I can't do that. My jobs..."

"Screw the jobs, Marilyn! From what you've told me, you don't care about them, anyway."

The drummer began a solo to tune his set. Jack and Marilyn didn't speak for a couple of minutes, the percussion detrimental to any conversation.

What the hell, she thought. Yeah, it could be fun. He seems nice enough. She didn't usually do this—take up with strangers in bars. But he looked harmless. And he might be a great diversion from her problems right now. A few days off the rock might be just what she needed.

Marilyn's voice rose to be heard over the drums: "What's the name of your boat?"

"The *Sea Cur*," he shouted.

"The *Seeker*?" she yelled back.

"Yeah," he shouted above the din. The *Sea Cur*.

"Good name. *Seeker*. I like that." It promised adventure. "So...what are you seeking?"

Strange thing to ask, he thought. Aloud he yelled, "A girl like you."

She brightened. The prospect had a lot of appeal. And Why not? Why the hell not? Meeting him here is no more dangerous than meeting someone on Tinder or eHarmony.

"We could sail to the Marquesas—or the Dry Tortugas. I've got snorkels and fins on the boat. Lots of food. Plenty to drink. A dingy for going ashore."

He could see the idea appealed to her but worried that she was wavering. "We could even sneak over to Havana. Would you like that?"

The musicians were all on stage now, and the piano player was attacking the keys with energy and élan. More partiers were drifting in off Duval Street, their talking and laughing adding to the din as the place filled up.

Finally, she looked at him and nodded. "You're right," she said above the noise. "I do need a break. I deserve one. I hate those jobs anyway. If they won't take me back after I go AWOL, to hell with them."

He patted her arm. "Good girl," he shouted over the blaring piano and drumming. "I'll settle up and we can head over."

"I have to go home and get my stuff first."

"What stuff?"

"Y'know. All my shit. Phone charger. Make-up, clean underwear, bathing suit. My passport if we're going to Havana..."

"But...but you won't need them."

"Toothbrush, dental floss..."

"You won't need any of that stuff," said Jack truthfully as she got up from the bar stool. He felt her pulling away from the web he'd so carefully spun.

She waved away his protests. "My bike's just outside and my place isn't far from here. I'll meet you at your slip in half an hour."

With a sigh, he agreed. "Okay," he yelled. He signaled for the check and got out his credit card.

The whole band was starting to play now, and its sounds were deafening.

"I'll wait for you on the boat. Don't forget—The *Sea Cur*."

"The *Seeker*, right! See you shortly."

And she hurried off as the band broke into Supertramp's "Good-bye Stranger."

Whipped Cream

by BJ Condike

Maria sighed. "I really love Doug," she said, as she dreamily stared at the bartender at the far end of the bar.

She was attractive in a wholesome, earthy way—not skinny like some of the anorexic babes we'd seen that day, but not overweight, either. Her yellow-and-black striped, stretchy tube top barely contained her ample bosom. She looked like a bumblebee chock full of honey. Brunette locks brushed bare shoulders of tanned, freckled skin. More skin peeked out between her top and her cutoff shorts. One long leg crossed its mate and dangled from the barstool; her feet loosely adorned with strappy sandals. Almond eyes gazed at the last few ounces of her margarita, and she let out a second sigh.

"So wha's wrong with that?" I said. "Love can be good thing." She had spoken to me since I sat next to her, and I felt obliged to be polite and respond. I didn't want to get into a deep conversation with this woman. My wife Mary Lou had gone to the restroom, and even in my inebriated condition I knew her to be sensitive about these things.

"He doesn't even know I exist," she pouted. "I come here all the time, and he pays me no more attention than any of these other chickees." She spit the last word. "I've had enough. I'm going home tomorrow. For good."

"Where's home?"

"Michigan. I came here three years ago on a winter vacation, and never left."

Maria was the fourth person in two days we had met with a similar story. A tourist would arrive and succumb to Key West's charms. The island's slow pace, campy bars, and balmy weather united in a siren call to escape the rat race of the frozen north. He or she would call home, have a friend or relative sell their belongings, and send them the money. They adopted a Bohemian lifestyle, worked hand-to-mouth jobs in the tourist trade, and lived for sunsets and beach parties. It seemed Maria was luckier than most—she had a real job as a bookkeeper for the local school system.

Doug the bartender slid up to us with an infectious grin. "Another round of 'ritas for everyone?" He wore a towel draped over one shoulder, and a bottle opener on his belt. His white polo shirt and green shorts revealed the battle stains and wet spots from tending bar like a flamboyant juggler. This was a man not afraid to work in the trenches, sloshing and splashing at will.

"Everyone" included our two traveling companions, Rick and Donna, plus an additional couple from Buffalo they had met at the bar. Doug also included Maria in our group, as well as the fellow sitting on the other side of her, another local known to both Doug and Maria. I didn't catch his name. I'm not sure he threw it.

We all agreed more drinks were in order.

"This round is on Jimmy," Doug declared, not for the first time. We'd been at Jimmy Buffett's Margaritaville for several hours and thought every fourth or fifth round being on the house was a good policy. Maybe it was just Doug engendering customer goodwill for a larger tip, but we liked it all the same.

Doug was a local celebrity. While skin diving a year ago, he had found a World War II practice mine and had brought it home. He used the porcupined object as a doorstop on his front porch and proudly showed it off to all who visited. He even had a framed photo of himself hanging over the bar showing him holding the object.

The Navy heard about the unexploded ordnance, and they were not pleased. News of the UXO hit the airwaves. Shore Patrol officers flooded the area around his home. Firefighters evacuated the neighborhood and police cordoned off the streets. The Navy's Explosive Ordnance Detachment arrived and set to work. The EOD team excavated a hole in Doug's front yard, placed the mine and a brick of C-4 plastic explosive in the pit, and covered the hole with a 10"-thick, steel-reinforced rubber blast mat.

The detonation resulted in noise ranging from a loud boom to a thudding whump, depending upon one's distance from the explosion. While no windows were broken, a cloud of dust blanketed the nearby homes and Doug's prized bougainvillea never recovered. The Navy used the operation as a public teaching moment about the dangers of UXO, and the local press idolized the dashing bartender in a front-page article complete with a photo of his perfect smile and bushy hair.

Which is where we first laid eyes on Doug—on the front page of the local paper we found when we checked into our hotel rooms. The incident only occurred a week ago, and Doug's fifteen minutes of fame had yet to fade.

We might not have made the connection had the young bartender not had a copy of the paper propped up on the bar. Our friend Donna saw it, and immediately wanted photos of us with the handsome barkeep. Doug was only too happy to oblige.

Doug returned with our drinks. I had to admit he was a looker. Wavy brown hair bleached by the sun topped a tall and slender frame. He danced behind the bar, mixing drinks with flair, whisking away the dead soldiers with a flourish. His smile made one feel he genuinely cared about you. Everyone, apparently, except Maria.

Doug left us and headed to the opposite end, not paying Maria any special attention.

Maria and the guy next to her sat on the short edge of the bar, just around the bend, facing the pit's long axis where Doug traveled between patrons. She had a morose look on her face, when suddenly she yelled, "Hey Doug!" down the alley of the bar pit.

Maria lifted her tube top and briefly flashed her bare breasts in his direction, grinning hugely. Doug glanced over his shoulder but failed to see the display before it ended. Everyone else in our group did, as evidenced by our gaping mouths and slack jaws. I checked with Rick, and he affirmed we indeed were in Key West and not New Orleans. Just then, Mary Lou returned and sat down.

"Yur not gonna b'lieve wha' happened," I said, and I told her.

Mary Lou peered over at Maria and replied, "You're right. I don't believe it. You've had too much to drink."

"No, really! Yesh, I had lots of 'ritas, but it did too happen. Ask Rick and Donna."

Our traveling companions confirmed my story, but Mary Lou still shook her head in disbelief.

Then Maria exposed her breasts again. "Hey, Doug!" she called. Still receiving no response, she repeated the action. "Dougie...!" she yelled. Doug turned and finally took notice. He raised his eyebrows to the ceiling and with a big smile used the two-fingers-to-the-eyes "I see you" gesture.

Whipped Cream

"What is going on here?" Mary Lou's mouth sagged open and caught some flies while it all sank in.

At that point, a conga line started on the main floor to the tune of one of Jimmy Buffet's songs. Buffett's original bar boasted loads of glass and brass, along with a kitschy island décor. Tables on a mezzanine level overlooked the main action below.

Uncounted rounds of margaritas caused us to stagger off and join the fun, snaking around tables and up and down stairs, brazenly hanging on to the hips of strangers as they wiggled their behinds in our faces. By the time we returned, thirsty and gasping, things between Doug and Maria had progressed several levels higher.

Maria's tube top was down around her waist. She supported her breasts with both hands over the bar top while the young barkeep produced a can of Redi Whip and squirted some on her bare right breast. Maria was all smiles. He proceeded to remove the white confection with his tongue.

The second time he covered both breasts and drizzled drops of Grand Marnier over the topping. Both he and the fellow sitting next to Maria enjoyed mouthing off the alcoholic garnish, one on either mammary. Maria tossed her head back and emitted squeals of delight. The crowd at the bar accompanied this activity with a variety of hoots, howls, and applause.

I will admit to a sweet tooth and was strategically positioned next to the aforementioned right breast, but Mary Lou glared at me.

"Don't even think about it," she said.

"What?" I grinned. So near, yet so far.

I could no longer say the word, "margarita"—it kept coming out "margarootie"—so Mary Lou decided we had had enough hedonistic debauchery for the evening. She grabbed my hand and dragged me back to the hotel.

Rick and Donna stayed for more fun and games. We did have one incident on the walk back, when a street sign seemed to jump out in front of Mary Lou without warning, causing her to walk directly into it, producing an egg-shaped lump on her forehead. We both agreed the street sign had been rude and disrespectful.

It was noon the next day before we were up and human. We met Rick and Donna for a late brunch and discussed the previous evening's events. We asked Donna about a purple bruise on her forehead. Apparently, a rogue street sign had come out of nowhere on their stroll home, and she walked into it. We told her it could happen to anybody.

We visited Margaritaville one more time before we returned home. Neither Doug nor Maria was there. I like to think she never went back to Michigan, that they live together in Key West, and that Doug keeps his can of Redi Whip at home.

Sunday Key West Artisan Market
A KW Indie Writer's Tale

by Janette Byron Stone

Put up tent
Takes we four
Height a must
Wind and rain.
Lay books out
Set the chair
Sit selves down
Big wait starts.
Daydream time
Palm fronds sway
Big white shark
Slinked
here
from
Great Aussie
Bight

Janette Byron Stone

Selling books,
Getting looks
Here she comes
Slow her down
Trip him up?
Pick it up,
Put it down
Be back later,
Useless line
Know it well
What it means
No hurt feelings
Be back later
Hm, not likely.
Better
You
Just
Walk on by hi hi
Like Dionne croons.
Still,
Try we must
Hawking
All
Our
Tales of scoundrels
Scenes in words
Memories past.
A concatenation
Of
Words in covers
Thoughts of lovers
Evil schemers
Playful dreamers.

Sunday Key West Artisan Market – A KW Indie Writer's Tale

"We wrote
These
Masterpieces.
Do you
Read?
How're you today?
Where you from?
Two for one
Best deal in town."

Words our bait
Hook like fish
Sink like weight
Open mouth
Keep it shut
Foolish pride
Is all that I have left
So let me hide
The tears and the heartache
You gave me
When you said goodbye
Oh walk on...

Hours pass
Not all bad
Mimosa calls
By god it's hot!
Talk too much
Blabber on
Engrossed in tales
Old friends now
Talk some more.
And then...

Janette Byron Stone

End of shift,
Pack and lug
Five books lighter
Dollars brighter
Could be worse
Nothing's lost
Meeting folks
Thawing out.
Two weeks' time
Try again
Heck, why not?
Never know
Brand new face
Choose that book.
Joyce is here
In walks Tom
Tent comes down
Mimosa time
End of day
Two weeks' hence
See you thence
Walk on by
Hm Hm Hm Hm Hm

Exit

by Earl Smith

Here's what you need to know about me. My name's John. I spent three decades as a CIA field operative. Unlike some of my traveling companions, I survived to retirement. What I did during those years is reserved for other stories, which may or may not be told. What's important for this tale is that I developed a reputation as a trusted go-between. As one friend put it, an ethical and personable assassin. Most of the opposition came to trust me.

After I retired, I became a neutral. Severed contacts with all actives. That's the rule, and it's never to be broken. I'd made a lot of friends. Traveled down some rocky roads. I missed the adrenaline rush. But the 'for God and country' thing had worn thin. Years of dodging, deceiving, and denying, and too many close calls had taken their toll. I happily faded into "context".

You may be wondering what's involved in retiring from the great game. It's called "re-virginelization." You were a virgin, then you got deflowered and then you get re-flowered. Like none of it ever happened.

Trust me, it's nothing like retiring from an advertising agency or a manufacturing job. It's much more convoluted. The first challenge is to convince everybody still in the game that you're really on your way out. And that includes the people on your side. They will see you as a resource to call on in a pinch while the opposition will wonder if you are a sleeper waiting for the right moment to pounce.

And then there are the habits that have become unconscious reflexes. In the decades I played the game, I developed lots of them. Training, field experience, and the demise of other operatives that screwed up—lost focus—drove what is called trade craft deeply into my soul until it became the very definition of who I was.

When you work undercover, you learn to hide those habits. That's what separates the good operatives from the rest. They're practicing trade craft. But even the most experienced player would be challenged to notice. Good operatives are dangerous poker players.

Here's a couple examples. When an operative enters a room, they scan systematically for threats and allies. Now, with amateurs, that's easy to spot. But an experienced professional gets it done without drawing notice. The eyes and head move independently. Barely noticeable distraction and subtle misdirection come into play.

Choosing where to sit in a public place is another example. Most operatives tend to sit with their backs to the wall and with a commanding view of the room. That makes them easy to spot. But a good operative might sit at a table towards the middle of a restaurant and depend on usefully positioned mirrors to cover entrances and exits.

One of the hardest habits to break is checking for tails. A good operative, and that means one who not only survives but prevails, is always aware of everything going on around them. And that includes knowing when they are being followed. There are many tradecraft tricks for spotting tales. And the pros know all of them. Reprogramming yourself not to notice is a real challenge.

Earl Smith

It means walking blind, knowing you are walking blind and truly being unconcerned.

When you become a neutral, you must stop practicing trade craft completely. That's a tough habit to break. The training becomes habits. Habits become reflexes. Reflex becomes instinct. But now you must stand in the open, vulnerable, and unprotected. You go from "I can kill you and you won't even see it coming" to "I won't even try to protect myself from you". The only way to get out is to drop your guard—a guard that has kept you alive—and surrender to whatever comes.

When you first announce your intentions to leave the game, all sides set out to test you. That's allowed by general agreement. You're followed, observed, and challenged. And not just by the opposition. The road to becoming a neutral is littered with potholes. If you're observed doing certain things, that will tag you as a faux neutral. That means you're still in the game and only pretending to be out. And that makes you fair game.

The initial testing can last anywhere up to two years. It depends on the senior players on all relevant sides reaching an agreement. All must accept you as a neutral before you are designated one.

But it's not over once you are declared a neutral. I still get tested on a regular basis. Maybe an impromptu contact from an old friend who is still in the game. Or an open tail, one which is purposely made obvious. Each time the response is the same, no tradecraft, no recognition, and no response. What goes on in the game has become irrelevant to me. I take no notice.

Then there are the times, often when I'm alone at night, when the memories come back. All the close calls and adrenaline rushes. I get to wondering what my old pals are up to. What kind of missions are they on? Are they even still alive? How many funerals did I miss?

Exit

Nostalgia is a dangerous traveling companion at those times. But I survived its many-headed assaults and, after ten months of testing, got my neutral ticket punched by a unanimous vote. That was over five years ago.

A generous retirement package, and certain ill-gotten gains, provide me with a comfortable lifestyle. I have a penthouse atop a brownstone on West 23rd Street in the Chelsea section of Manhattan. My neighbors think I'm retired from some government agency and working on writing my memoir. I spend a lot of time in Key West. Ying and Yang. My life is well balanced and, more than occasionally, delightful. But more on that later. And nobody has tried to kill me for years.

I was in Manhattan when this tale begins, just stepping out of the shower. Looking forward to what promised to be a delightful evening with the personal assistant to the French ambassador. Life was good, and I was enjoying the anticipation. Then the phone rang.

"John, you got a minute?"

I recognized the voice immediately. One I shouldn't be hearing. As far as I knew, Ralph was still an active. Still in the game. The rules were clear and everybody, on all sides, accepted them. I would drop off the board, become a neutral, and no active would ever, under any circumstances, contact me. The knot growing in my stomach told me to offer an obscenity and hang up. But Ralph had, on more than one occasion, saved my ass. And my instincts were telling me that this was not a test.

"I'll assume you have a damn good reason for this," I responded. "You know the rules. No contacts. So, unless you've left the field, and, as far as I know, you haven't, this had better be a matter of life or death—mine!"

"It's a matter of life or death. But not yours," Ralph replied. "I'm not calling on my own. And I'm not looking to scuttle your retirement. You know me better than that.

Earl Smith

"There's an agreement amongst certain parties that a meeting between you and me will be allowed and that you'll remain a neutral after it's over. No matter what you decide. Just to be clear, I'm not going to propose anything that'll reactivate you. If you want further information, I can't provide it over the phone. I just ask you to trust me. You willing to meet?"

When the guy on the other end of the line pulled you out of the path of a bullet, you tend to feel you owe him. Of all the people I'd known during my active years, Ralph was the one I was most likely to trust. He knew that, and he knew that I knew that. So, I didn't hesitate. "Okay, one meeting. In public. Where and when?"

"Le Sans Culotte in twenty minutes?"

"I can see you haven't changed. You're the same presumptuous bastard. You're on the island! You son of a bitch. You assumed that I would agree to a meeting. I have a date tonight with an assistant to the French ambassador and you know how much I like French women. I'm going to give you this one. It damn well better be worth it. Make it an hour. I've got to get dressed and do some serious groveling."

My next call was not a happy one. Monique and I had been spending time together for over a year. She had a femininity that I was attracted to. I'd been planning to invite her to spend some time in Key West. She wore a bikini well and nothing at all even better.

She knew how to flirt. Was devilishly good at it. A playfulness that most American women find either difficult or threatening. Mostly, I suspect, because of American men. I liked her and she liked me. And, as far as I knew, she'd never killed anybody.

Monique knew me well enough to hear something in my voice. "You're not backsliding on me, are you?"

238

Exit

Long and short, she said she understood but I knew she didn't. I had to promise Paris in April and Christmas in Key West to get things settled. As much my gain as hers. I was smiling when I hung up. But that quickly turned to a scowl.

I put on casual and grabbed a cab to the upper east side. Le Sans Culotte is one of those undiscovered Manhattan gems. None of the entrées are worth eating, but they serve an incredible sausage rack with a wide range of cheeses and freshly baked bread. The wine list is first rate. Major league grub. It's so special that Manhattanites never tell tourists about it.

Ralph was there when I arrived. Sitting at a table in the middle of the restaurant. I almost smiled at his consideration because I knew he would rather be sitting against the wall next to the rear exit. But I didn't smile. I was irritated and confused. "Okay, I'm here. Now tell me why I'm looking at you instead of a very winsome woman. And, assuming you're still an active, why the hell are we meeting?"

"We have a problem. You remember Svetlana?"

That name brought memories flooding back. She was a brilliant, and ruthless, Russian field operative. We nicknamed her Sweat because she could make any man sweat without breaking one herself. She was a member of the double-digit club. That means over ten kills. You stop counting after ten. It's considered bragging.

Some years ago, one of my mentors told me something that saved my life multiple times, including times with Sweat. "Some women are too dangerous to be considered beautiful." She was one of them.

"Yeah," I said. "The only people who don't remember her are the ones who didn't survive. So why do you ask?"

"And I'm sure you remember Bob Stephenson."

"Okay, is this a memory test? What's your problem?"

"Our problem is the two of them. And when I say our, I include a bunch of sides. She's a very important and effective operative who carries a lot of sensitive information between those pretty ears. The Russians have invested heaps of rubles in her and are not happy about the possibility of losing their investment. Bob is now driving a desk, having been recently promoted to get him out of the field. The two of them are, how shall I say it, one. They want out together. Become neutrals, get married, maybe have kids, and live normal lives. It's the pillow talk that has everybody concerned. And the possible tell-all book. Jesus John, a top Russian operative and a senior American agent. Do you wonder why everybody's freaking out?"

"Then you do have a problem. But what's it got to do with me?"

"We need an arranger. A negotiator. Not a mediator but an arbitrator. Someone who can navigate the shoals and reefs. That all sides trust. Someone to guarantee the results will hold. For what it's worth, all parties trust you. There's no second choice we could agree on. We need your help to either untangle this mess or eliminate the problem short of eliminating the two of them. You'll travel in the open. No cover."

Ralph got a serious look on his face. His voice seemed to drop an octave. "One of two things will happen. If you decline, this meeting will never have happened. You'll go back to the life you've been living. Sanctions will be issued. Problems solved. If you decide to play, they'll have a chance. But I'll need you in Key West ASAP.

"You'll still be a neutral. Anyone who moves against you will be immediately sanctioned and removed.

Exit

You'll be classified immortal. Every side will see no harm comes to you. Your word binds any resolution once it's signed off by all. Key West will be designated a temporary neutral ground, much like Vienna during the Cold War, and you'll be interim King of the Conch Republic. You'll have three days to sort it out." He paused and looked hard into my eyes. "If you want time to think about it, take as much as you need, as long as it's within the next hour."

I smiled and shook my head. "You already know I'm not going to turn you down. But I'm going to need a few things. First, unquestioned sanction ability. If I say take 'em out, covered quick and no excuses. Second, a safehouse on the island that I will own free and clear. A compound that can be secured. I get to choose, and no questions asked. Third, a secure net that'll allow me to instantly contact any of the parties. Fourth, unrestricted funding for my team and the compound. And I pick the team. Fifth, anyone who finds their way into my company is automatically under my protection. They'll be untouchable as long as they stay on Key West or until I remove my protection. Finally, if I'm successful, designation of the island as permanently neutral ground. I'll be permanent reigning King of the Conch Republic. I may think of more, but that's it for now. Can you cover those?"

Ralph nodded and offered his hand. I decided that was good enough. As we were shaking, I gripped hard and said, "One more thing. I'm not going to this dance naked."

"Your old kit will be made available. The Walther, knives, vest, taser, explosives, electronics, docs, and the rest. Updated, of course. If you need more, you'll get it. No questions asked. I'll tell everybody I had to give that to get you onboard."

You might wonder why I was willing to try to save a Russian operative who might have, at one time, tried to kill me. By the way, she did try. I was just a tad faster. She who shines brightly, the translation of Svetlana's name, was a potent adversary. But something grew up between us over the years. A mutual respect and deference developed. She had standards and ethics I admired. Not just in it for the blood. We had both held back when... Well, that's another story and above your current paygrade.

Bob was an old friend. We had planned and executed missions together. I was godfather to his oldest son and helped him through when his wife and youngest were killed in a car accident. If the two of them were in love, I was enough of a romantic to want to help.

"Okay, you got me. I need to get cracking. Make some arrangements."

Ralph slid over a package. A private jet at JFK, suite reserved at my favorite hotel, a fat stack of Franklins, one of those special no-limit credit cards, a secure burner phone, and a briefing folder marked "eyes only."

"Strictly observed restrictions," Ralph said. "No weapons other than yours, no collateral players, no covert actions. No contacts with sympatico locals by anyone. No intermural negotiations. It all goes through you. You're the only game in town. Ringmaster in the big top. No surveillance. All out in the open. Cut the deal and get them out or we will."

We spent the next half hour going over the setup. The Russians, the Americans, and, for some reason, the Brits. Sweat and Bob were already on the island. As were the three delegations. Everybody would stay in their lanes until I gave clearance. Particularly the two of them. All nicely arranged, and a clear indication that Ralph had anticipated my decision. This time, I didn't mind as much. I almost smiled.

A limo was waiting for me outside Le Sans Culotte. I headed for the airport, settled into a plush leather Gulfstream seat, inventoried my kit, reviewed the briefing folder, and flew down to the Conch Republic.

The folder was interesting to say the least. The Russians were holed up Gulf side at the Marker on William. The Americans were on the other end of the island at The Reach. The Brits were at the Pier House at the foot of Duval. All nicely separated.

They put Sweat up at the Duval House, keeping her close to where I'd be staying. A clear indication they thought that she was going to be the biggest challenge. And likely volatile. Lost her cool once and two dropped. As my old mentor said, "Some women..."

Bob was banished to the Harborside Motel & Marina. Located on Eisenhower, it's above White on the Gulf side. Nice digs but a bit out of the way. There was no possibility they didn't know they were both on Key West. But, given what was at stake, I figured they'd behave.

The Key West airport was its same old welcoming self. Normally, I breathe more easily down here. Something in the air or the mojitos. But this time it felt more like 'out of the shower and into the swamp'. That knot in my gut had not completely gone away.

I settled into a suite at the La Concha. It's on Duval between Eaton and Fleming. Centrally located in Old Town and superbly run. I wanted to head down to the Green Parrot and drown my cares in a pool of mojitos and the ear-numbing sound that always spills out onto the sidewalk when the band is in full stride. But instead, I spent two hours organizing a schedule for the next day. Early morning coffee with Sweat at Freda's. The Russians at the coffee shop at the Marker. Down to the other end of Duval for drinks with the Americans at the Café at the Mansion. Back up Duval for Pimm's cups with the Brits. Then up to Harborside for a late lunch with Bob. Just enough time with each for me to lay down the law and let them have their say and no more.

Around ten thirty, with the schedule set, I headed down to the hotel wine bar. I got a glass of a nice Merlot, a selection of cheese and meats, and headed to a table in the back. I'd just settled in, when things got serious. A Bozo walked in wearing too much. In Key West, the only reason you wear too much is to hide things. I tagged him as an active and probably Chechen or Russian. My hand drifted towards the Walther. But I caught myself. "Easy now. You're a neutral." It was time to trust Ralph.

Bozo did the Jekyll and Hyde thing that is always a dead giveaway. He came through the door with purpose then quickly shifted into casual mode. This guy had clearly been to school, but tradecraft had yet to become instinct. If your target is a very experienced operative, being that sloppy can be hazardous to your health.

Clearly not a front-line pro, Bozo was giving away way too much. He paused, looked around, made me, and then, much too casually, began to move toward the bar.

He didn't get very far. Three guys in more appropriate clothing entered right behind him, one on each side and one at his back. The one on the left pressed the point of a shiv against Bozo's ribs and whispered something. Bozo turned pale. The four of them about-faced in unison and left. The guy trailing looked in my direction and winked. I figured their new friend would make it halfway to Cuba.

Back in the room and an hour later, my burner phone buzzed. "I understand you almost had a visitor," Ralph said with a chuckle. "The guy's a Russian. Part of the crowd that wants the old Soviet Union back. Can't stomach détente with the West. A Putin puppy. Believe it or not, when we searched his room, we found an autographed photo of Tucker Carlson. You'll be honored to know that the team that took him out was two Russians and a Brit. Cooperation is flowering in Key West. There may be more of these guys wandering around, so we'll watch your six. I'll stay close." So, Ralph was going to take a hand. I slept easier.

The next morning, I headed for Freda's. It's one of those hidden Key West gems. Marcia, the major domo, welcomed me like returning family. Svetlana was already there. Sitting at a table in the back of the garden. She looked tired and sent me a hard stare. "So, you're the one who's going to decide my fate," she said.

"Let's cut through the bullshit. There's no time for it. You really don't want us to get off on the wrong foot," I responded sharply. "We both know it's mostly up to you and Bob. I'm here to see if things can be worked out. You can believe it or not, but I'm on your side. Now tell me how it is." We spent the next half hour probing. Sweat was tentative at first. Not like her at all. But she gradually opened up. We had never talked human-to-human that way. Both of us always hid our feelings. The break came when she asked me about my life as a neutral and I mentioned Monique. "I never danced. She makes me dance. I never played the flirting game. We flirt all the time. But mostly, I never truly relaxed with someone else. Monique won't tolerate me not relaxing. French women can be so bitchy when they're frustrated. And so amazing when they're not. You see, I do understand something of what you're reaching for. I have a bit of it myself."

She stood up, bent over, and kissed me on each cheek. "I put my fate in your hands."

We shared a hug. I headed out. My major take-away was she was deeply in love with Bob and was going to jump ship whether I got things worked out or not. She was hard-defiant. We reached an understanding. No action until I had my try at working things out. That was a major win in my book. I headed to the Marker.

The Russians were overflowing with indignation and concern. Paranoia is the national disease and they had it bad. First, it was this person is too valuable an asset. Then came we don't confirm that this person is part of our operation. Then, we have invested too much in her to let her go. And we will not take the risk. Russian logic is always a challenge to westerners. Around and around, they went. Making less sense each time. Two things were clear. First, they were going to be a loose cannon in this. Second, they had no real remit. No firm guidance from above. Unpredictable and unable to make any binding agreement without the approval of their superiors.

Russian bureaucracy, particularly in the intelligence field, is heavily top down and slow to forgive failure. If a field operative screws up, a trip back to Moscow can prove right uncomfortable. These guys were clearly making that kind of calculation. But they didn't appear to have any solid guidance and they knew their superiors came in two varieties. The poor bastards didn't have any good options. It was damned if they do and damned if they don't. No matter what they decided, Siberia was a real possibility.

Finally, Russian fatalism settled in. And that's how I left it. I headed out with little confidence that they would play along with whatever I came up with.

I headed up Duval. It was time to farm a more fertile field. Halfway along, I spotted Ralph on the opposite side of the street. He was looking in the window of Shadow and Fish, one of the better clothing shops on the island. His overt presence was a solid indication something was in the wind.

Exit

I kept to the plan. No sign of recognition. No trade craft. Not my problem. It would be taken care of. Later I learned that my tail was an errant fragment of the Russian group. Apparently, the senior member. He picked me up along Duval and was tailing me in an attempt to find his guy. The one that got halfway to Cuba. I hear, this one is now a resident of Gitmo.

I arrived at the Café at the Mansion unaccompanied. Michael, the owner, had reserved my favorite table on the porch of the hotel. Right up front, it has a magnificent view of the Atlantic, a nice sand beach, the pool, and plenty of scantily clad ladies. He gave me a questioning look and, when I grinned, shook his head, shrugged, and walked away.

The Americans were already there and well into morning libation. I was hoping Ralph and rum had prepared the ground for me. They were mostly resigned to the situation. "We're not happy about this, but it's probably going to happen. Bob deserves a chance. But, if you can't work things out, we will have no choice." Not all I wanted, but enough to feel more optimistic.

The Brits were the surprise. "We have side-access to both. It will be tough to lose that. No, we haven't turned them. Just discrete channels. Bob has mostly gone offline, but Svetlana is still useful to us." They ended up in the same place as the Americans. Resigned acceptance.

By the time I got to Bob at Harborside, three things were clear. First, Sweat was determined to get out and be with Bob. Second, nobody was happy with the possibilities and risks. Third, the Russians were still not onboard. But I did have a hole card to play with them.

Bob was careful at first. But he made it clear what he wanted. Both were irretrievably committed to each other. Nothing was remotely as important to them as getting out and becoming neutrals. I left lunch with a plate of snakes that defied untangling.

The balance of the afternoon was spent with an agent from Caldwell Banker. Her eyes got big when I described what I wanted. Visions of a fat commission danced in her head. When I said the purchase would be cash, she glowed with anticipation. Probably figured I was either laundering Russian money or investing for some Wall Street hedge fund. I didn't disabuse her from either assumption.

We looked at a couple of places before getting to one on Southard, just below White. It was perfect. Five bedrooms in the main house and a separate guest cottage. Pool, hot tub, cabana, a porch that ran all around the second story of the main house. Set back from the road with a gatehouse. The look on her face, when I offered full price and handed over my credit card, was the cherry on the sundae. She called the owner. Closing was set for seven days.

Back at the hotel, I called Ralph. Told him I'd badly raided the treasury. "Bought it nuts, guts, and feathers. Furniture, golf carts, and all. But I'll need to redo the bedrooms. I'll forward the invoices. Get the tech guys ready to do their thing. Tell the Russians, Brits, and our guys. Give them the address and make sure they agree it's holy ground." He didn't even ask what it cost. "I'll get the geeks on it day after closing," was all he said.

I was a new homeowner with a problem. Needed time to think. So, I headed down to Mallory Square. The bartender at El Meson de Pepe's saw me coming and had my mojito ready by the time I arrived. I love that bar. Its outside with a great view of the channel and Sunset Key. Two hours, several mojitos, and a plate of great coconut shrimp later, I was heading back up Duval with nothing that even remotely approximated a solution. Two lovers against the national security interests of at least three countries. I needed a nap.

I have this ability to let my mind off leash. Let it roam without explaining itself. I showered, hit the rack, and told it, "You figure it out, I'm tired." I was asleep as soon as my head hit the pillow.

Then came the dream. I was walking along a white sand beach. There was a gentle breeze. Warm sunshine. Up ahead, Monique was coming out of the water and waving. The water drops on her bikini sparkled in the sunlight. Her smile warmed me with anticipation. We lounged beneath palm trees, ate, and drank. Talked and flirted. Later, we made love. As we lay close together, she whispered, "No one nor nothing could keep us apart, my love."

My eyes opened and I stared at the ceiling fan. Gradually it came to me. I realized it wasn't Monique or me on that beach. It was them. We were just stand-ins. And what Monique said was what they'd been saying to me. The truth at the core of this conundrum wasn't all the risks that the Russians, Brits, or Americans were worried about. The risk – the very big risk – was that Svetlana or Bob would do something that would put the other's life in jeopardy. And that was a risk that neither one of them would ever take. The solution was clear. I didn't need to guarantee anything. The way they were committed to each other was rock solid insurance.

The next morning, I was on a mission. My first stop was the Russians. "Look guys, we've been acting as if we have a choice. They're going over the side whether we approve or not. I don't think we have to worry as much as we've been. Their commitment to each other is solid. There's no chance they will do anything to put either of them at risk. We need to trust in that. I suggest we make the best of the situation. Let's not piss off the orangutan."

I told them about Bozo and his journey halfway to Cuba. The picture of Tucker Carlson. The background of the Putin puppy. And how it all wove into a dangerous tapestry heavily populated with mines. It was clear they already knew some of what I told them. After all, their guys were involved in stopping Bozo from getting to me. And then I played my hole card. The tail on Duval. I made the point hard. If they didn't play along, there were elements of their own intelligence organization that would force their way into the lead.

"So, what do you propose, my friend," the senior guy asked? I laid out my deal. It took half an hour. When I finished, they headed off to another table and had a heated discussion in Russian. They seem to have forgotten that I spoke the language. Or maybe they just wanted me to overhear. My hole card had clearly worked. They were worried about getting pushed aside for some geopolitical agenda.

The long and short of it was the final decision was not theirs to make, and they were trying to decide to whom to pass the hot potato. When they got back to my table, they told me that they appreciated my suggestion, and would discuss it with their superiors. When I left, I figured there was only half a chance that they would go along with anything I worked out.

As I headed up Duval, I rang Ralph and gave him a sitrep. I told him what my proposed solution was. He laughed when I got to the part about the dream. "I'll have to meet this Monique sometime," he said, "she must really be something to get your attention that hard."

"I'll make sure that never happens," I said with a chuckle. "But let's get back to the core problem. The Russians could scupper this. There's no telling who they're going to contact for approval. If we get the right guy, things could work out. But if they go to one of Putin's

Exit

puppies, it could trash the whole thing. By the way, was I tailed?"

"Yep. The handler for Bozo. He had a heart attack right there on Duval. Well, it looked like a heart attack. Luckily an ambulance was handy. One of ours. The EMTs were quick to realize that his malady was more than the local hospital could handle, so he got shipped to a US government facility in Cuba. You stay your course and I'll make some calls. I've got some outstanding favors that I'm going to call in. See if you can get the other four in the box and I'll manage the Russians.

The Americans and the Brits were a much easier sell. And without the drama or the need to consult higher-ups. Both groups accepted that there was absolutely no chance that Svetlana and Bob would stay in. They were out. Playing as if they weren't was just stupid. In the end they agreed that the best way forward was to manage their exit. Let them become neutrals. And that the risk of any downside was manageable. By the end of the day, two parties had signed off on my proposal. The Russians were still the unknown. But that was Ralph's problem. It was time to bring the two at the center of all this together and lay it out for them.

I made reservations for dinner at Café Solé on Southard. It's one of my favorite eateries. The hogfish is not to be believed. They arrived together looking nervous. I laid it out for them. "Okay, here's the deal. You'll spend six months completely isolated on an island off the north coast of Cuba. An associate of mine has an arrangement with the Cuban government. She has done favors for them. You won't be prisoners but, trust me, there's no good way off the island. You can leave at any time but, if you do leave, the deal is off. And you know what'll happen next." They both nodded.

"Then you'll spend an unspecified time at my house in Key West. You'll be classified temporary neutrals. You'll have no contact with any active. You'll report any attempted contact to me, and I'll handle them. No traps or tricks. We won't try to ensnare you. After I'm satisfied, I'll recommend that you be classified permanent neutrals. If all sides agree, you can go your way. Wherever that is, no one will know but me. That's the deal. If you don't like it, you can try on your own. But that's the best I can offer. Don't make me look bad in front of the children. Take it or leave it. Now!" Sweat smiled and nodded. Bob pulled her closer. My burner phone rang, and I walked to the bar.

"The Russians are on board," Ralph said. "It took some doing, but they eventually recognized the realities. What turned them was my guarantee that Sweat, and Bob were going to operate under the combined protection of the others involved and that, if any of their operatives attempted to take them out, they would be dealt with. To their core, Russians are fatalists. They decided to honor their national tendency. How's your end going?"

"Both have accepted my proposal and are looking relieved." I reviewed the deal with Ralph just to make sure we were on the same page. The bartender tried to listen in but got bored. No juicy local gossip.

"Good on you. What do you need now?" Ralph asked.

"We are about to order dessert. Have the senior member of each side outside the Café Solé in half an hour. I'll outline the deal, and each should be ready to acknowledge the arrangement and indicate they have accepted it. I'll take it from there."

Four were waiting for us when we left the restaurant. Ralph, and one from each side. I told them the deal was cut and described it. Each said it was accepted, that they would abide by its terms, and all shook hands. Even the Russian was cordial.

As of this writing, the two of them are on the Cuban island. I hear their decision to start a family may be underway. At least that's what the visiting gynecologist told me. They'll be arriving at the safe house in a couple months.

Two attempts were made to contact Sweat. She immediately reported them, and the situations were resolved in a public way that assured no further foolishness.

As for me, I'm spending nine months of the year on Key West. The island has been declared permanent neutral ground. The compound has been fully wired. There's a Chinese couple that serves as chef and gardener. The guard shack is manned twenty-four seven. My neighbors are not sure what's going on but, in Key West, people are not overly nosy, especially if you throw good parties.

Monique resigned her job and moved in. Her tan is outrageous. No lines. I've added two more women to the team. Both retired operatives and far too dangerous to be considered beautiful.

The four of us are living in the main house. I'm still a neutral and immortal. Ralph tells me that there may be other exits ahead.

Author Bios

Author Bios

Rodney L. Aldrich

Rodney Aldrich is a poetry and prose writer who lives in Troy, New York. One of his poems was published in the Isotope journal. He won first prize for poetry in the "Exaggerate!" media contest sponsored by The Arts Guild of Old Forge, Inc. He has traveled to Ireland thirteen times to assist peace makers in the reconciliation process from their civil war. He is an environmental engineer who is committed to humanity dealing with the slow motion, ongoing, and worsening climate crisis.

Bernie Bleske

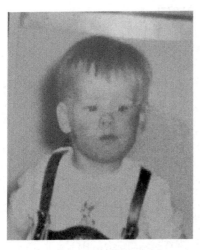

Bernie Bleske dropped out of college in Wisconsin over 30 years ago, intending to move to Key West and pursue some life unrelated to being a professional adult. As if living in another century, it took him two years to get here. (Long stories involving old car disasters in minus 60-degree weather, sensible course reversals followed by senseless decisions, hard-learned truths about money, and so on and so forth.) Within a year of arrival, he met a local girl, a 4th generation Conch, who consented to marriage on the condition he leave the island and become a professional adult. Some years, degrees, careers, children, and locations around the planet later, he and his wife returned to Key West.

Bleske now attempts to teach 8th graders some history and sporadically writes on **Medium** (**BernieBleske@Medium.com**) and other places.

Joanna Brady (Schmida)

Joanna Brady (Schmida) came to Key West from Canada twenty-seven years ago after a successful career in Advertising. As a feature writer for the Key West Citizen and later, Konk-Life newspapers, she has published two novels, an historical novel of Key West, ***The Woman at the Light*** (St. Martin's Press, 2012) and more recently, ***Night Witch in Berlin*** about a Russian woman bomber pilot in post-WWII Berlin. She has won awards for them, as well as for her entertaining short stories.

Elia Chepaitis

Elia Chepaitis lives on Grassy Key, and also in Machiasport, Maine and Westbrook, Connecticut.
The author is a former newspaper columnist for the New Haven Register, a recipient of three Fulbright fellowships, and a professor emeritus of information systems who invented an alternative to Braille before turning to a life of crime with novels such as *Murder with Kayaks in the Florida Keys* and *The Murders on Cayo Costa*.

BJ Condike

Brian "BJ" Condike originally hailed from New England, but after spending a quarter century in North Texas he now resides in Big Pine Key, just spitting distance from Key West. BJ's favorite genres are mystery and science fiction.

BJ minored in English while pursuing a BS in chemistry at UMass Amherst, and later earned his MBA. Most recently he graduated from The Writers Path at Southwestern Methodist University in Dallas.

BJ loves writing short stories and has won several regional contests. He also placed in the top 1% in two national contests by Writers Digest, each with over 2,000 entries. His short stories have appeared in several anthologies, including **_Strange & Sweet_** (2019), **_Malice in Dallas – Metroplex Mysteries Volume 1_** (2022), and **_Tall Tales and Timeless Stories_** (2022).

BJ spent ten years acting and directing in community theater, and thinks realistic dialogue is key to a good story. "When you're on stage," he says, "dialogue is all you have."
BJ is a member of Mystery Writers of America, Sisters in Crime, and the Key West Writers Guild. He is currently revising his first novel, _Murder is Personal_. Read more about BJ at **www.BJCondike.com**.

ML Condike

ML Condike completed the Southern Methodist University's Writer's Path in Dallas in 2019 and was invited to participate in a New York Seminar along with twelve other writers in the program.

ML's short stories appear in anthologies that include ***Strange & Sweet, Stories from the Granbury Writers' Bloc*** (2019), ***Tall Tales and Timeless Stories***, Granbury Writers Bloc (2022), ***Malice in Dallas, Metroplex Mysteries, Volume 1***, Sisters in Crime Anthology (2022).

"A Cowgirl Farewell" won first place in the fifteenth annual Writer's Digest Popular Fiction Awards, Mystery/Crime category (2019). "The Yellow Poster" won 2nd Place in the Tennessee Williams Short Story Contest, Key West Art & Historical Society (2022).

ML is an associate member of Mystery Writers of America Florida Chapter, Sisters in Crime National, Sisters in Crime North Dallas, Granbury Writers' Bloc, and Key West Writers Guild.

> Website: www.MLCondike.com
> Twitter Link: **ML Condike**
> Instagram Link: **ML Condike**
> LinkedIn Link: **ML Condike**
> Amazon Author Page: **ML Condike**

Dale Dapkins

Dale Dapkins - Won first Prize, Tennessee Williams short story contest. 2016. Grand prize in the Lorian Hemingway short story competition in 1999 and again in 2000. (First to win consecutively) Got a shout-out on NPR's Morning Edition for that one.

Dale's novels and short story collections include **_American Broccoli_**, **_Bad Billy Barracuda_**, **_Bird Boy_**, **_Blue Moon_**, **_Ebola, a novel_**, **_The Homeliest Angel and the Last Honeybee_**, **_Lincoln the Art Thief_**, **_The Lobster Boat_**, **_Maine Moose Dill Pickle_**, **_Prize Winners_**, and **_Yeti Porn: Island Stories_**.

Joanna Gray

Joanna Gray fell in love with Key West on her first visit in 2008. She joined the Guild shortly after she and her husband finally made the island their home in 2017, and settled in to teaching, writing, and crafting. Joanna's work has won the Key West Council for the Arts Writers Grant, has been published in *Decimos (We Say)*, and short listed in WOW's flash fiction contest. She serves as treasurer for the Key West Writers Guild, as well as a volunteer for the Key West Literary Seminar. She is a member of the Historical Novel Society and fishes with her husband on weekends, where she has mastered the art of telling fishtails.

For more information about Joanna, see her Google site
Joanna Gray Writes
(https://sites.google.com/view/joannagraywrites/home)

Contact: joannagraywrites@gmail.com

Author Bios

Rusty Hodgdon

Rusty is a graduate of Yale University where he majored in English Literature and Creative Writing. After graduating with a Juris Doctor degree from the Boston University School of Law, he practiced law for over twenty years in the Boston area, first as a Public Defender, then with his own firm. He left the practice of law and moved to Key West, Florida to pursue his passion to write creative fiction. Rusty is the President of the Key West Writers Guild, the longest standing writers' group in Key West, and also the winner of the 2012 Key West Mystery Fest Short Story contest and the recipient of the Florida Keys Council of the Arts 2017 Writers Award. He has written six novels and one collection of short stories. All comments are welcome. Write to him at: Rusty.The.Writer@gmail.com

Jennifer Juniper

Jennifer Juniper's love of travel mixes well with her uncontrollable curiosity—leading to adventure and intrigue. Pulling from life experience, she chronicles connections and inspiring interactions. Her essay **"A Father By My Name"** was a finalist in WOW! Women on Writing. An excerpt **"The Fish Doctor"** from her upcoming memoir was recently published. Her poetry is featured in ***But You Don't Look Sick: The Real Life Adventures of Fibro Bitches, Lupus Warriors, and other Superheroes Battling Invisible Illness***. She is an award-winning poet currently living on the road with a kitty she was only supposed to foster, splitting her time between here, there, and everywhere while working on her memoir *Gut Instincts*.

Jennifer blogs at **Solo Chick Traveler**. Website: **www.jenjuniper.com**

Laura Knight

Laura Knight grew up in Northern Michigan and lived in South America before moving to Miami with her husband. The memory of her Miami sojourn endured through fifteen moves, one son, countless cats and dogs, and careers ranging from radio sales to physical therapy.

Laura Knight credits the Key West Writers Guild for sharpening her skills and encouraging her to publish her first book, ***Third Court: Memoir of a Miami Neighborhood***, an engaging snapshot of a diverse Miami neighborhood in the late 1970s. Her flash fiction has been published in *Decimos—We Say*. Readers of this anthology will discover what Guild members already know—the people and geography of the Keys offer endless inspiration for all creative endeavors.

Lesa McComas

Lesa McComas - One of the first generation of women Surface Warfare Officers in the U.S. Navy, Lesa retired from the Navy after 20 years and her second career as a defense analyst. She earned a Master of Science in operations analysis from the U.S. Naval Postgraduate School in Monterey, California, and a Bachelor of Arts in biology from Franklin and Marshall College in Lancaster, Pennsylvania.

Lesa is has coauthored/authored the last three editions of ***The Naval Officer's Guide***, a textbook for prospective Naval Officers published by Naval Institute Press, and was a regularly featured columnist in *Navy Times*. Lesa and her husband divide their time between Key West, Florida, and their summer home in "Pennsyltucky."

Josie Mintz

Josie Mintz was born and raised in South Florida and spent most of her childhood outdoors and barefoot. Her passion for travel and adventure has taken her to the other side of the globe and back. The places she's been and the people she's met along the way are seeds in the fertile soil of her imagination. She has written a number of short plays that were performed locally.

Josie is also a visual artist and holds an MA from the University of Chicago. After a time focused on academic writing, Josie is grateful for the opportunity to pursue her first love—creative writing—in Key West, the place she feels most at home. Josie currently lives on a boat with her husband, daughter, and an 8-pound Havanese who labors under the delusion that he is a Rottweiler.

Dick Moody

Dick Moody is an artist, illustrator, designer, art director, sculptor, author and a professional saxophone player—Rock, R&B, Country, and Jazz. He has been a member of the Key West Writers Guild for several years and a resident of Key West for thirty-one years.

Dick has published two adult fiction books on Amazon Kindle under his pen name **Richard Saxbee**, namely ***Good Girl – Bad Girl***, and, ***How to Get in Trouble in Key West*** He is in the process of writing twenty-four short stories for "Antidotes from Life".

Five pages of his artwork may be found on his website **www.dickmoody.com**–

Dick spends one week a month in Tavares, Florida with his wife and teenage granddaughter.

Linda L. Moore

In "Poinciana's Tears", **Linda** writes about her grief as it comes and goes in waves following the death of her beloved nephew. It is her first published piece of creative nonfiction. Linda's writing talents grew from poetry and evolved from there with a degree in mass communication and journalism from the University of Wisconsin-Milwaukee. She has worked as a public relations writer, a freelance journalist and a technical writer. In 2008 she left her job to live and travel the Caribbean Islands on a sailboat with her husband.

In addition to writing the sailing blog, **Sailing Troubadour**, Linda's articles about the sailing life have appeared in *Southwinds Magazine*. In 2020 she dipped her fingers into the fiction genre and wrote three short stories which were published online at **_Short Fiction Break_ shortfictionbreak.com:** **_The Chain Saw and the Cherry Tree_**, **_Stories from the Boundless Project_** and **_Fallen_**.

Linda continues to live on her sailboat in Key West. She is honored to be a member of the Key West Writers Guild and is working on a memoir.

Katrina H. Nichols

Katrina Nichols writes poetry, flash fiction, and memoir pieces. She is a storyteller at heart, hard at work on her family memoirs, which span four generations. Her collection of stories, all passed down to her as first-person history, will be called ***Twice Told Tales***.

Katrina's writing career began at the campus newspaper at Temple University while she earned a degree in Journalism. She has worked as reporter at *The Daily Local News* in West Chester, PA and more recently, as a copywriter and editor for small businesses.

She first visited Key West in 1978 on a family vacation and felt the magical pull of the island. She returned several times before making Key West her home from 2018 - 2021. She now splits her time between her home state of Pennsylvania and visits to Key West. Katrina remains an active member of the Key West Writer's Guild and served as President from 2020 to 2021. She is now a board member and runs the Zoom portion of the meetings.

When she is not writing, Katrina enjoys reading, spending time with friends, and most of all anything outdoors with her children, Daphne and Torin.

https://www.linkedin.com/in/katrinanichols/
http://www.KatrinaNichols.com
https://www.facebook.com/katrina.h.nichols

Amber Nolan

Amber Nolan is a restless travel writer who calls Key West home. Her work has appeared in *USA Today*, *Frommers*, *Tripsavvy*, and several other travel publications. Amber's most unusual project involved hitchhiking on small airplanes to 49 states, during which time she spent two years on the road, or rather, "on the skyways."

She is a recipient of the 2020 Anne McKee Artist's Fund for her book, **Wingin' It**, which documents the unusual journey and provides insight into the aviation community.

Amber also worked as an investigative reporter for *Key West the Newspaper* (the Blue Paper) and has a bachelor's degree in journalism. She's currently a sustainability writer and editor, film production assistant, and screenwriter.

Visit her website at **AmberNolan.com**

Mia Shawn

Mia Shawn - Presently I am living and writing upon this little Island of Key West. I just concluded my first visit to another island, the home of my ancestors and bards, Ireland in September 2022. Like Ireland, poetry in Key West proclaims Her subjects, and celebrates Her profound literary treasures. Writing poetry and stories since childhood, my muse was nascent by necessity in early adulthood. Pragmatic, ~ supporting myself and family. First published in the regional publication for the Keys, "DECIMOS"; stage actress and radio productions with Fringe Theatre of Key West, and local playwright, Ms. Toby Armour; member of the Key West Writers' Guild and Key West Poetry Guild; member and active with the Key West National Organization for Women; and more. My spirit, grounded in science and environmental protection, now sings skyward as it embraces the Arts of this little Island. This is the first publication of my poems here in this Anthology. Written in, and celebrating, Key West. They are only the beginning..."

~ Mia Shawn, October 2022.

Earl Smith

Earl Smith lives in Southwest Washington, DC. He is the author of several paranormal, action-adventure novels. The Cabal Series includes: ***The Broadway Murders***, ***Assault on Omega***, and ***The Sound of Fury***. ***Response***, a political thriller, is the first in the John Reynolds series. *Dream Walk* is a series of Zen parables. Earl writes both fiction and poetry drawn from his life experiences. He received a PhD in Political and Social Theory from Strathclyde University in Glasgow, Scotland, an MMS from the Sloan School at MIT, and a BA from the University of Texas. An itinerant, he has lived all over the world, played the great game (intelligence) internationally, founded six companies and two non-profits and lived in Manhattan for almost two decades. Now he wanders about and exhales stories and poems.

Jan Stone

Janette Byron Stone, M.Ed., satisfies her passion for literary expression by writing books, short stories, newspaper articles, ditties for those who inspire, and the occasional poem. She is the recipient of the 2022 Key West Writers Guild award for her work in progress "Prairie Lotus Flower," the Military Writers Society of America silver medal award for her debut ***Please Write: A Novel***, and the Florida Keys Writers Conference award for first page pitch. Other published works include ***Gifts from Time and Place***, a collection of short stories, essays, and vignettes, and "Alexis' Island: Growing Up in the Tropical Paradise of Key West," a look at life through the eyes of a ten-year-old boy living on a sailboat within dinghy distance of the island. Janette is fascinated by the lives of real people and the effect of actual events on history. It's no surprise she finds herself most at home writing in the genres of historical fiction and creative non-fiction. Currently her website is in reconstruction, but you can contact her at jcstone154@gmail.com. You'll also find her most Sundays in season with her Key West Writers' Guild friends selling books at the Artisan Market.

Patty Tiffany

Born in Appalachia, **Patty Tiffany** absorbed her poet grandmother's love of reading and writing, along with a reverence for nature and the rolling hills of home. Dreams of travel to the wider world came true first during her master's program in German, eventually allowing her to live in Mexico, Canada, Austria, and Germany. After 30 years in higher education, primarily as a dean of admission, Patty makes her home on a bight in Key West, where her home floats and sometimes rocks, whim to the fickle sea. She is a member of the Key West Writer's Guild and Poetry Guild. She is a 2022 winner of the Anne Mckee award to complete a second collection of her work, and her first poetry collection, Awoken, was published in 2019. Her work has also been published in *Danse Macabre*, *Decimos*, and several anthologies.

D.E. Triplett

Born and raised in Kentucky, **Duane Triplett** found his love for reading in the classics – *A Tale of Two Cities, Light in August, The Count of Monte Cristo* – though his delayed dream of becoming a published author was a long way off.

After receiving a degree in communications from the University of Florida, he worked at a local television station before attending law school at UF. Post-graduation, Duane worked as both a prosecutor and public defender before transitioning into court administration.

Once he discovered his love of the written word, Duane spent years honing his creative writing under the beautiful man, and Pulitzer Prize nominee, Janos Shoemyen (who wrote as Lawrence Dorr). Recently, his short story "The Santa Fe Street Critique Group: Spotting Blindspots" was a finalist in the Key West Literary Seminar's 2023 Cecelia Joyce Johnson Award contest.

As a recovering postmodernist author, Duane now lives in Key West, Florida with his anarchical dog Rex. When not toiling over a manuscript or curling up in a still-unpublished fetal position, he enjoys reading, watching movies, and telling tourists that he just saw Tennessee Williams holding Hemingway's hair back as he was throwing up on the other end of Duval Street.

Email: detriplett1@gmail.com

Arida Wright

Arida Wright is the CEO of Powerlines Publishing, LLC, President of Powerlines Healing by the Sea Ministries, a poet, and a published author. She lives her philosophy of self-empowerment, which for her is a lifelong mission of spirituality. She is a Minister of Metaphysics and a Traditional Reiki Master. Currently, she is a member of the Key West Writer's Guild and the Key West Poetry Guild. She is a past columnist for Key West the Blue Paper and Village Voices newspaper. She has a collection of poems in several anthologies. She is the author of the book **_Then Sings My Soul_** and soon to be published, **_Crossing the Threshold: Voice of a Black Woman_**.

Judi D. Winters

Judi Winters is a member of a declining species, a native New Yorker, and a community activist since kindergarten. Although tied to her roots, as a world traveler her thinking and writing embrace a global perspective. The origins of her far-flung blog are unlimited, stretching from the world's highest internet café on Mount Everest, across the Big Blue Pond, through the wilds of the Peruvian Amazon jungle, and even to several east-west and north-south road trips across America the Beautiful.

A compulsive storyteller, her thirst for knowledge and her desire to share these experiences is unquenchable. Her stories of adventure turned into multi-sensory travelogue presentations capture a wide-eyed and ever-widening audience. Relating anecdotes was a much-needed skill set for teaching severely emotionally disturbed children in NYC. Well-told stories held the students' interest and subtly conveyed curriculum goals.

Her first novel, *Adventures in Time*, was a fifth-grader's posthumous tribute to H.G. Wells and included sojourns to Topsy-Turvy Land and The Mushroom Planet. Several drafts of children's books, musicals, a two-hander comedy, and an adult picture book are projects-in-waiting. Winters' activism, enthusiasm, and lust for life may have begun in kindergarten but has served her in good stead into the Social Security years.

She thanks the Key West Writers Guild for their guidance and allowing her to hone her craft.

Author Bios

Made in the USA
Columbia, SC
09 December 2024

47648147R10161